WHEN WILLA FELL

a novel

Laraine F. Eddington

Cover design by: Joey Eddington
Library of Congress Control Number: 2018675309
Printed in the United States of America

*For my children; Rachael, Cody, Maxwell, Joey and Corinn.
You listened to every story and are willing to listen still.*

CONTENTS

PROLOGUE

I didn't plan on killing someone the year I turned twelve, let alone my best friend Willa. But in an instant, I learned that life and death and plans aren't even on speaking terms. And that was that. Done and dusted. I didn't plan on keeping it all a secret either, but owning up to what happened that day in the canyon felt like killing her all over again. And so the truth lay heavy and dark somewhere deep inside me, like a lump of lead slowly leaking out poison. Willa was dead. And now Willa's death was killing me.

CHAPTER ONE

October 1971

More cinnamon rolls

Gussie and Lizzie were squished beside me in the porch swing, blue plastic cups of cherry Kool-Aid sloshing as they rocked back and forth with uneven jerks. The wood creaked against the metal chain and our legs advanced and retreated in the weak autumn sun.

Gussie took a messy slurp, a red clown smile crawling up both sides of her mouth. She said "Lizzie, when we go back to kindergarten, I get to tell about Willa being dead for show and tell because I am the oldest."

"Hold on," Lizzie interrupted, her voice outraged. "That is so unfair!" She looked at me like I should be equally angry and asked, "Effie, who do you think should get to tell about Willa?"

I felt like I was going to bust out and scream like a banshee. Or punch them both in the face. Or maybe pour that Kool aid over their stupid heads. Something. Anything. Just so I didn't have to hear my little cousins brag for one more minute about having a dead sister. It was like tragedy gave them some special celebrity glow.

Willa is dead. The thought continued to shock me—a bubble rising from deep down inside me to pop into reality in my brain. It came with a fizz of shock like the stinging of tiny needles. I found myself whispering the words *Willa is dead*, over and over trying to make it real, trying to make mind soak it in. A best friend and cousin all rolled up in the package that was my life. Gone.

Gussie said" Okay Lizzie, listen, this is the deal. I will tell about Willa dying, I mean passing away, and then you can say..."

Lizzie finished Gussie's sentence "...because she had a horrible, terrible, accident."

Gussie changed her mind and shook her head. "Okay wait, now listen Lizzie and this is final. I am the oldest so I will tell about *how* Willa died, because that is the most important part."

"Oh great, so, I just get to say, 'Willa died 'and that's it?" Lizzie's blue eyes were blazing. "That is not even—at all."

Gussie said "Trust me Lizzie, everyone will feel really sad when you say that, and Miss Crandall will probably start crying."

I had been trying to be kind, and I knew they were only five, but jeez, I had definitely had it. The twins thought having a dead sister equaled being related to Elvis.

I stood up abruptly, jolting the swing backward and said "Shut up you guys. Show and tell is stupid so just shut up about it."

Lizzie looked at me, unoffended. Her big sister Willa had been telling her to shut up since she learned to talk. "Effie, did you and Willa like Miss Crandall when you guys were in kindergarten?"

Talking with the twins was like chasing a jackrabbit. You had to be ready to pivot fast in a whole different direction. But I was eager to talk about kindergarten if they would shut up for a second.

I sat down on the edge of the porch, my feet dangling in Aunt Holly's dying petunias I said "Yeah. We both really liked her."

Gussie kicked her chunky legs hard, pumping the swing. She said "But Miss Crandall's face is so scary, she looks like a melted candle."

"I know Miss Crandall is not pretty." I interrupted firmly, "But you won't even notice how she looks after a while."

"Not even all that jiggly skin on her neck?" Gussie shuddered.

I remembered everything about that first day of kindergarten; snuggling up close to Willa on the bus ride, clutching matching pencil boxes filled with dime store treasure; a 24 pack of perfect crayons, sharp and dangerous yellow number 2 pencils, and a pink eraser as soft and rubbery as a new baby. I lost my last bit of scared when Miss Crandall let Willa sit in the desk right next to me. This lasted only a week because we talked too much, but by then I felt like I'd been in kindergarten forever.

Gussie broke into my reverie "I asked Mom when we have to go back to school but she wouldn't tell me."

Lizzie said, "You're supposed to quit bugging her while she's resting Gussie." I wondered if Aunt Holly was ever going to get enough rest. She had turned into someone I didn't even know, someone who didn't make breakfast, lunch or dinner. Someone who put a blanket over her bedroom window to block out the light, someone who had turned into nothing more than quiet lump under the red and white star quilt on her bed.

A half mile away, a shiny new red pickup was passing my house on the narrow highway climbing the hill towards us. Who could be driving a spanking new Chevy? I couldn't think of anyone in our little town that got a new truck without my brother Jimmy Scott informing us about it in lots of boring detail.

Bill Decker was driving the truck that pulled up in a crunch of loose gravel at the edge of the lawn. Gussie and Lizzie jumped down from the porch swing in a rush and I put my hand out to hold them back. I said" Hold your horses there girls."

Bill and Minnie Decker raised Herefords on a ranch several miles to the east of us, and I had always admired their brand, which was a D inside of a diamond shape. Bill got out of the truck and came around to Minnie's side, where she handed him a foil covered cake pan through the window. She opened the door and swung her short legs around so they were sticking straight out the door, then eased down in short jerks until both feet hit the ground in a little puff of dust. She stood, getting her balance and fussing with her blue and white flowery house dress until Bill handed the pan back to her. He removed his John Deere cap as they walked towards us over the big front lawn. Smoothing a nervous hand over his short grey hair, Bill turned his head aside to spit sparingly on the lawn.

The twins broke away and raced toward the Deckers, thundering like Shetland ponies toward a feedbag. Gussie accidentally tripped Lizzie who landed flat on her belly, spilling her Kool-Aid. She picked herself up, unembarrassed. They came to a stop in front of the Deckers, blocking the path to the house, talking over each other in a flurry of words.

"Did you know our big sister Willa died?"

"Do you know that Willa got killed in the canyon?"

"It was a terrible, horrible accident."

"Come on, we'll let you see her, she's in the living room."

Lizzie grabbed Bill's arm and Gussie tugged on Minnie's. As they pulled toward the door, Lizzie said proudly, "And you can see Willa wearing a brand new dress in her brand new coffin!" Geez Louise she sounded like the announcer on "The Price is Right".

Minnie Decker paused at the front door and turned toward me. She pried Lizzie loose and leaned out and hugged me with one arm. Minnie smelled and felt like a fresh cinnamon roll. She said "I am so sorry you lost your cousin, Effie. I don't think I have ever seen you two girls when you weren't together. You might as well be twins like Gussie and Lizzie here. You've been best friends forever, haven't you?"

I nodded and managed to mumble around the lump in my throat, "Yeah. For our whole lives." We had both turned twelve this year.

Minnie squeezed me again and turned to the twins, "Can you girls take these rolls in the kitchen for me? I just took them out of the oven, and you might want to eat one while they're still warm." Gussie was the quickest, grabbing the pan and marching, elbows high, into the kitchen.

I plopped down on the grass and lay down on my back in the middle of the lawn, letting the autumn sun find my skin. I could feel the warmth. I could feel it right now, and Willa could not. How could she be lying in there, so separate from me? How could she not be sharing this feeling? How was I supposed to go through the rest of my life hearing the wind howl, smelling the rain rattling the juniper trees without Willa feeling it too? I wanted to back up a month, whirl backward in a time machine to start the school year over, when it had just been me and Willa. Before Verna came. Before the Canyon.

CHAPTER TWO

One month earlier, September 1971

Bad news

It was like being trapped in hell, held captive by the devil. Our kitchen was hot and the windows were opaque with steam from two big enamel kettles boiling away. The yellow formica table was cluttered with mason jars, some empty and some full of bottled tomatoes. Gross—they looked like bloody little body parts. The worn gold linoleum was sticky underfoot and the whole scene was exhausting. I was wasting my Saturday bottling gore with the devil.

The demon holding me trapped was my mother, who actually looked didn't look too satanic, although her muslin apron was splattered with blood red tomato sauce and her short hair wilted down the sides of her pretty face in brown strands. It didn't matter to her that I had just survived a week of sixth grade that had lasted at least a month. It was Saturday for Pete's sake. I should have been galloping bareback on old Lightning, or building a fort with Willa, or any of a million fun things instead of fishing stupid tomatoes out of a gigantic pot of boiling water while sweating like a pig. I plopped another red blob into the cold water in the sink. Things were depressing enough, and then Mom dropped the A-bomb. I didn't even see it coming.

"Effie, I need to talk to you about something." Mom began with her back to me, her voice pitched up a couple notches with cheeriness I immediately suspected.

It hit me then. This" something" was going to stink like a road kill skunk. I just didn't know it was going to ruin my whole life.

She turned around and wiped her hands on her apron. "Your Dad and I have decided that our family should take in a Navajo girl from the reservation during the school year."

I dropped a hot tomato into the sink with a splash and said "What do you mean 'take in'?"

Pulling a slimy skin away with the edge of her knife, mom cut a tomato in neat halves in her palm and slipped each half into a glass jar, rounded side out. She continued. "I mean she will be living with us until next summer, going to school with you."

"This school year—you mean *now*?" my voice was outraged.

"Yes." Mom said, peeling another tomato and avoiding my deadly skinny-eyed stare.

She continued "I know this is really springing it on you, but we had to make a decision today. They were counting on a foster home that has fallen through, and your Dad and I both feel like this is something we can and *should* do."

A million angry thoughts churned in my brain. I didn't know where to start. I said "Holy crap Mom, don't they have schools on the reservation?"

Mom said, "Don't say crap, Effie. Of course they do, but…"

I didn't wait to hear her excuse. "Why us?"

She tried to sound reasonable "Well, we have room, and…"

I interrupted "What do you mean, 'we have room'? Hey, wait a minute." My voice went all squeaky, like a cartoon mouse. This happens whenever I'm out of control and about to cry. I really hate it. I blurted "Is she going to sleep with me? I have the littlest bedroom. Jimmy Scott's is way bigger than mine."

Mom turned away, drying her hands on a soggy towel and said, "Oh Effie, don't be ridiculous. Of course she'll share your room. You have a nice double bed and we're going to put another dresser in there and it will be just fine." Mom's voice had the twang of barbed wire being tightened on a new fence. I knew it was useless, but I couldn't help myself.

I said "Why do *we* need to do this? Why can't they find someone else?"

Mom said "Because she needs a place right now. She is already a week behind in school. Besides it won't hurt our family one little bit to help out someone in need."

She pushed a strand of hair back from her damp forehead and put her hands on my shoulders, turning me around. I kept my eyes on the floor but she lifted my chin so I had to look at her. "Effie, it will be fun for you to have another girl around. Like having a sister! "

I said "I don't need a sister. I have Willa and she's way better than a sister."

Mom went on as if she hadn't heard me. "Her name is Verna and she is in sixth grade, just like you. Won't it be great to have someone who is always here to talk to and do things with?"

"I am not sleeping with a dang Indian." The ugly words were out before I even knew I was going to say them.

I knew I had gone too far. The barbed wire in Mom's voice snapped and I could hear the zing. "Young lady, you go directly to your room and don't come out until I tell you." She took a step toward me, her face tight with fury. I took a step backward, banging my leg on a chair. She continued, her voice deliberate " On second thought, you skedaddle right out to the chicken coop and clean out every nest, shovel out every scrap of chicken manure and old straw. Then put new straw in. I don't want to see you until the coop is clean enough for a picnic with the president."

It took three hours full of dust, chicken poop and futile tears before I finally finished. I didn't ask permission, just slipped the hook in the door of the coop and left, starting up the long hill to Willa's to tell her the bad news. I knew she would be just as mad as I wanted her to be. She was that kind of friend.

CHAPTER THREE

Jello in the cellar

I began to run as soon as my feet left the driveway. I never walked when I could run; my legs wouldn't let me. Today outrage gave me wings.

The sky sprawled huge and blue overhead making everything below seem small. I down the side of the highway, past scrubby creosote bushes, my new black Converse 'kicking up red puffs of dust. Creosote bushes aren't anything particularly worth your notice until it rains. A northern Arizona thunderstorm pelting on a Creosote bush will rattle loose a pure rainy smell sweeter than you could ever dream up.

When I was little, the distance between Willa's house and mine seemed like a journey across the world, but now that I was twelve it was nothing. The first part of my run was easy and my body felt light. I tried not to slow down, but when I passed the halfway tree I was breathing hard. The old juniper was a quarter mile from both our houses, our meeting spot. Junipers have prickly green bunches on the branches instead of leaves and chalky blue berries. Their twisty trunks look a million years old with shaggy bark that you can peel off in strips. They have a sharp, clean smell I love—like Christmas.

I crossed the lawn and jumped over Aunt Holly's petunias, climbing the steps to the porch held up with peeled and varnished posts. The ranch house was long and low, roofed with graying cedar shakes. I didn't knock of course. Knocking on my cousin's front door would have been as loco as knocking on my own.

Calling, "Anybody home?" I smelled something horribly familiar.

"In here Effie girl—back in the kitchen." My Aunt Holly's voice floated from the back of the house.

I went through the entry way to the kitchen. There was a basket of tomatoes on an oilcloth covered table along with a couple dozen quarts already full and cooling on red and white striped dish towels. Water was boiling in a dented silver pot and there was a plastic bucket full of slimy tomato skins on the floor. It was the same disgusting scene of horror I had just run away from. Aunt Holly was at the sink washing mason jars in front of a steamy window.

She said "Why Effie, how nice of you to grace our home with your lovely presence."

I said "Hi Aunt Holly. My Mom's doing tomatoes too." Aunt Holly laughed and pushed up her smudgy glasses with her birdie finger. She was so innocent. She probably didn't even know that meant the F-word. She said "You sneaked off did you? Lila's probably on the phone calling a posse to hog-tie you and bring you back home." I breathed a sigh of relief. Obviously Mom hadn't called yet to tell her I was in disgrace.

I loved my Aunt Holly. She is what my dad called "cheeky" and laughed a lot. She didn't spend her whole day worrying about how I was going to turn out like my Mom did. She liked books as much as I did, and had even named Willa after a famous author, one she told me I'd enjoy when I was older. Even though they were really old, she had lent me all her Laura Ingalls Wilder books and we both agreed that "The Long Winter" was the best one. I also suspected Aunt Holly knew nearly every word in her big fat dictionary; except maybe the cuss words, but that was okay because Uncle Slab knew all of those. Also, Aunt Holly put real chocolate chips in her cookies, not pathetically healthy carob chips like my mom did.

She was my mom's younger sister by nearly ten years. Mom got married when she was old and Aunt Holly got married when she was young. This meant Willa and I were born at the same time. We even got born on the same day—June 18th, 1960. It gave me shivers to think what a big waste of friendship it would have been if it hadn't worked out that way. I thought probably Mom and Aunt Holly liked each other almost as much as Willa and I did.

I said "Where's Willa?"

Aunt Holly held up a finger as she filled a glass with water from the tap and took a long drink, finishing with an audible smack. "Oh don't you worry Effie girl. I've been working her ever since breakfast. I sent her down to the cellar to get me some more bottles."

I said "I have something very important to tell her." My eyes smarted instantly with tears that came from nowhere.

"Oh?" Aunt Holly cocked her head and her eyebrow went up.

"It's the worst news ever." I said.

She said "Something ghastly?"

I nodded mutely.

She gave my shoulder a pat and said "Well for heaven's sake go get it off your chest, but don't forget my bottles."

The splintery wood screen door slammed behind me, causing Uncle Kitty to lift his head and glare at me with hateful eyes from the back porch. Uncle Kitty was older than I am and bigger than cats should be allowed from gorging on mice in Uncle Slab's barn. His ears were gnawed to nubs from some kittenhood trauma. I ignored him and headed for the cellar.

Willa's cellar was the old-fashioned kind, dug underground and not attached to the house. The plywood door was lying open in the dirt. This gave me an idea. I grabbed the silver handle with both hands and swung the door over, lowering it quietly until it closed. Just before it shut I heard thumping sounds on the steps, bottles clinking and Willa yelling. "Hey, knock it off...I'm down here, someone's down here!"

I waited a second and then pulled the door back open again and laid it back on the dirt. Willa was already near the top of the wooden steps, a box of mason jars in her arms.

She said "Effie, you jackass. You scared the hell out of me. I had already pulled off the light." Willa's new hobby was cussing, especially because she knew it cracked me up.

I bent over laughing and pointed. "Your face, you should see your face."

Bottles rattled as Willa plunked them down on the lawn, sending a half-hearted kick at me. She said "I'll get you back, don't think I won't."

I wiped my eyes on the sleeve of my t-shirt. I always cried when I laughed hard, just like my Dad. It was so annoying to cry when I was both happy and sad. Was anyone else like this, or was I a freak? I said "I'm sorry Willa, I just saw the door open and..." I straightened up and sniffed. "Honest, I am really sorry Willa. Don't be mad. And anyway I've got something horrible to tell you. You are seriously *not* going to believe."

Willa looked interested. She loved bad news. She said "C'mon, let's go back down. I could use some jello."

We creaked back down the steps and Willa waved her hand in the air until she batted the string and yanked on the light bulb dangling from the ceiling. The cellar was cool and the dirt smelled delicious—sweet, like apples. The swinging light sent rays back and forth across shelves lined with Aunt Holly's hard work. There were bottled green beans, pickled beets the color of rubies, applesauce laced with cinnamon, spicy taco sauce, tomatoes, pale golden peaches, apple pie filling with nutmeg and crab apple jelly. There were white plastic buckets of wheat, ready to be ground into breakfast mush or flour for wheat bread. Aunt Holly's cellar always gave me a safe feeling.

Willa's hand hovered over the boxes of jello lined up on the shelf. She said" You choose— cherry or orange. There isn't any lime."

I said "Cherry's okay" and held out my palm. Willa poured a pink anthill and I stuck my tongue in it. The tangy sweetness made my mouth flood with spit.

Willa sat down on a bucket of wheat and said "So what's the horrible news?

We sat there, licking jello and I told her everything, a bond of hatred for the Navajo girl growing between us, sweet as cherry jello.

CHAPTER FOUR

Stinky grenades

Willa came over after church for dinner so she would be on time to watch my life get ruined. After the pineapple upside down cake she helped me dry the dishes. Jimmy Scott was asleep on the living room couch with the funnies across his chest. Willa held a finger to her lips and nodded. I smiled, reading her mind like usual. We sneaked down the hall easing the door open into Jimmy Scott's bedroom. Spying on my teenage brother was a constant thrill.

"Holy cow, it stinks in here" Willa hissed, plugging her nose.

I sniffed. "No kidding. It smells like milking boots, Hai Karate and B.O." Willa clamped a hand over her mouth to hold back a snort of laughter. I whispered, "Mom makes Jimmy Scott keep his door closed so it won't contaminate the rest of the house." She had given up on reforming him.

"Who in the heck are these guys?" Willa walked over to a poster tacked on the wall. There were three long haired men in front of a tree; one of them with a beard.

Casually, like I knew what I was talking about I said, "Oh that's Creedence Clearwater Revival, they're really popular." I really didn't know if they were popular or not, but they must be if they had their own poster. "Jimmy Scott calls them CCR."

Willa said "Man, for a cowboy, Jimmy Scott sure likes hippie music."

I said "I know. It drives dad totally crazy."

Jimmy Scott's room was full of piles; dirty clothes in the closet next to an empty laundry basket—a pile of clean clothes unfolding on the bed. Books were stacked in a messy pile in the bookcase and piles of dusty vinyl records covered the lid of his old stereo.

I said "Hey Willa, want to see if he has any new love notes?" as I pulled at the top drawer of his dresser. It was heavy and rattled, full of odds and ends like shards of Indian pottery, pennies, empty juicy fruit wrappers and .22 bullets.

Picking up a piece of folded up blue-lined notebook paper Willa said, "Is this a new one?"

I said "Open it up and let's see." We heard steps in the hall and the door started to open. Willa froze in horror but I snatched the note from her hand, dropped it in the drawer and turned around, pushing it closed it behind my back.

Jimmy Scott came slouching into the room, scratching at an armpit. He had grown about six inches in six months and his backbone didn't seem to be keeping up with the rest of him. My brother had turned ornery when he hurt his knee and had to quit football. In our little town, playing football was the only way to prove you weren't a loser. Now, instead of football practice he had more time for chores. It was not a good trade. Lately, his life seemed to be one miserable day after the other. The only thing that cheered him up were cheeseburgers and Geraldine on the Flip Wilson Show.

He took a threatening step towards us, eyes sweeping the room. "What are you little creeps doing in here? You're not supposed to be in my room."

We began inching toward the door. I said "We were just..."

He growled "You better not be messing with my stuff. Get out of here before I pound you."

We edged past him, only turning our backs when we were out the bedroom door. Giggling wildly we ran through the kitchen, out the back door and into the barn, collapsing on a hay bale.

"My heart is beating so fast." Willa gasped with her hand on her chest.

I was laughing so hard I could hardly speak, "That...was... so...close."

I lay back on the scratchy bale and pulled a piece of hay out to chew on it while my heart slowed. Reed thin columns of sunlight sliced through barn wall cracks, lazy dust motes floating. The roof was high above me, ridged tin sheets lying on the trusses. The floor below the stacked bales was a spongy mixture of hay and dirt. Our barn was big, built before I was born. It had a two story rectangular shape, and was the only blue barn around. Mom told Dad it was a fine present to have a barn painted in her honor, just because blue was her favorite color. The barn walls were fading like old Levis, the boards traced with silver ridges.

There was a small door in the long side of the barn that faced the house, with a tack room for saddles and bridles just inside on the right. Big stacks of crisscrossed hay bales rose on the other side of the door. The chicken coop took up the far end of the barn. A long row of mangers and watering troughs bordered the other long wall, with separate pens open to the outside for our cow and the horses. The loft was built above the pens, providing shade over the mangers. Two massive doors were at the end of the barn opposite the chicken coop, ready to swing open when the hay truck needed to be unloaded.

Willa scratched her ankle, which was sprinkled with freckles like the rest of her. "What do you want to do now?"

"Um...How about we hunt some eggs? I said, "Maybe Mom will let us make brownies."

Mom's ignorant hens were supposed to lay their eggs in the comfy little chicken apartments Dad made. But our chickens didn't believe in the easy life. I didn't know how they could be both so dumb *and* so tricky. Gathering eggs was a treasure hunt.

We started with the cracks between the hay bales. Willa stretched her arm down as far as it would go. Her voice was muffled, "How do they even get down here?"

I said "I have no clue. The eggs probably squish right out their bums when they climb in."

"Hang on, I think I feel something." Willa brought three eggs up one by one.

We climbed the ladder to the loft and I found two more eggs behind a piece of rusty farm equipment. When I turned around Willa was bent over an old wringer wash tub, the top half of her body buried inside. She pulled out with a grunt. "Hey, check these out Effie. They look really old." She had an egg in each hand, each one mottled with tan spots.

I eyed them dubiously. "Do you think they're rotten?"

"They have to be." The evil glint in Willa's eyes meant that she had thought of something fun and risky. "Let's take them out in the field."

"How many are there?" I asked.

"Six, no seven" Willa's voice was muffled again as she dove back inside the washer.

I climbed down the ladder. "Here, hand them to me." Willa carefully handed down one egg at a time. We left the good eggs in the barn and gingerly carried the rotten eggs out to the field.

As we crossed the weedy irrigation ditch inspiration struck. Willa said "How about we pretend these are grenades? What's that Indian girl's name again? " I crouched in the ditch and then popped up and lobbed at our new enemy. "Take that Verna Yazzie!" An instant wave of smell hit as the rotten egg exploded in the field. It made me want to gag.

"Holy Cow, that reeks!" Willa plugged her nose with her left hand and lobbed another one out with her right. It arced high into the air and hit the ground with a huge smelly splat. She yelled "We'll never surrender Verna Yazzie!" A hazy stink settled over us as we took turns lobbing eggs.

The screen door slammed and Jimmy yelled "Effie!" We

ducked back into the ditch, giggling. There was a pause. "What is that?" Jimmy sounded disgusted. "It smells like crap out here."

Laughing, I popped out of the ditch. "Uh, just some rotten eggs we were getting rid of."

Jimmy said, turning back into the house. "Well get in here. Someone just pulled in and mom thinks it's that girl."

We climbed out of the ditch, swatting dust off our jeans. "Great," I frowned at Willa, "You might as well shoot me because my life is now officially over."

CHAPTER FIVE

Verna sure doesn't talk much

Mom was peeking out the curtain at the Ford pickup in our driveway. She said" James, I'm sure that's them, but they're just sitting there." Dad walked over, opened the front door.and gestured, "C'mon Lila, they must be waiting for us to go to them." We followed dad on to the porch and, sure enough, the truck door opened as we walked down the steps.

I was very curious to see what Verna and her parents looked like. I didn't know any Indians first hand, even though I had grown up in Arizona. We had the Navajo Reservation to the north of us and the Apache Reservation to the south. We were pretty much surrounded.

Mrs. Yazzie stepped down from the truck first, a tiny woman with skin the color of milky cocoa. She was wearing a deep red velvet blouse and a pink skirt that fell in crinkly layers like a birthday cake. Turquoise earrings dangled from her ears and her dark hair was pulled back and wrapped with white string in a bundle low on her neck.

Verna's father was wearing a spotless white straw cowboy hat, a plaid western shirt with pearl snaps on the pockets and black Wrangler jeans. His wide leather belt was pressed with fancy designs and had a silver belt buckle with a large turquoise in the middle. Actually, except for that cool belt buckle, he dressed a lot like my Dad.

Finally, Verna climbed out of the truck. Straight black hair fell forward and covered her face as she looked down at the ground.

Her hair was cut in severe lines; one across her forehead just above her eyes and another at the bottom a few inches above her shoulders. She was pretty scrawny. Sizing her up, I decided I could beat her up if I needed to.

Stepping forward Mom put out her hand to say hello to Mrs. Yazzie, but quickly pulled it back because Mrs. Yazzie was looking at the ground and didn't see it. Looking at the ground must be a Navajo tradition. When Mrs. Yazzie finally answered my Mother, she spoke so softly we could hardly hear her. She sounded uncomfortable speaking in English. I couldn't keep myself from staring. What was that between her eyebrows? It was a small blue letter "N". Holy smokes, it was a tattoo! I elbowed Willa and pointed at it, using my Mom as a screen. I didn't know anyone with a tattoo except LuDean, the town barber, who had been in the Navy. Willa and I exchanged a look. This family was exotic.

Shaking hands with Mr. Yazzie, Dad asked him about their trip. He introduced himself and Mom and then said, "And this must be Verna. We are so glad to meet you." He gestured to me. "Effie, come on over here and meet Verna."

I took a step forward and said, "Oh hi," which sounded really dumb but I had no idea how to act. What was I supposed to say to someone I had never met before who was going to be sleeping in my room and invading my life? Suddenly I realized I was going to have to change clothes in front of her from now on. The thought made my face go hot and I was glad no one could read my mind.

Mom and Dad invited everyone to come in the house and visit, but Mr. Yazzie said they had to get going. Opening the tailgate he got out a beat up pink suitcase and a cardboard box that said Jim Beam. We looked away as the Yazzies hugged Verna and said brief goodbyes. They spoke Navajo in low tones which sounded a million times different than English. Mrs. Yazzie's face settled into sad lines as she climbed back in the truck.

After a couple tries, the engine started and the Maroon Ford pulled back on the dirt road. I could see a sticker that said "Indian Power" on the bumper as they headed north toward Luka-chukai. Verna didn't wave but stood in the driveway, looking after them for a long time.

She finally turned to follow me into the house and I showed her around. She didn't say one single word, even when I showed my bedroom, which I had been cleaning like crazy. I began to wonder if she understood English.

CHAPTER SIX

Dad puts his foot in it

The whole family took Verna on a tour of the barn, where she was first introduced to our milk cow, Bell. Dad walked to the next stall and said, "And these are the horses. Verna, do you like to ride?"

Verna, gazing steadily at her toes, finally giving her answer, a shoulder lifted up in a half inch shrug.

Encouraged, Dad scooped his hand into the rolled oats and held out a flat palm. "This big red gelding is the horse I ride. We named him Lightning because he was born in a lightning and thunderstorm, right out there in the pasture. You may not want to try him just yet, unless you have ridden horses a lot." Lightning delicately munched away, staring at Verna like the rest of us.

Verna said nothing, but she had lifted her head slightly and was peeking through her bangs at the horses, so I knew she was interested. She lifted her head a little more. Golly she had a lot of big white teeth! It looked like she had a few spares. They crowded forward pushing against her lips.

Dad continued "And this is our mare Missy and her little filly, Callie. Callie was born last March and she is going to be a beautiful horse, don't you think?"

It was like talking to a wall.

Dad took off his cowboy hat and scratched his head. He wasn't giving up. "Now this here is a horse you will enjoy riding.

We call him Navvy, because..." Uh oh, suddenly Dad remembered why we called him Navvy. I could not wait to see how he got out of this one.

"Uh, we call him Navvy because we bought him at an auction." Dad continued in an extra hearty voice, way too enthusiastic. I looked at Willa and rolled my eyes. He plowed on "Yup, in fact we bought him in your neck of the woods, yesirree, right up there at a big auction in Window Rock, right there on the reservation. As I recall, we bought him from a real fine Navajo man. Yup, that's right. And he has been a wonderful horse, just as well broken and gentle a horse as you could want." Finally running out of steam he said in a pleading tone, "Effie loves to ride him, don't you Effie?"

I tried to sound bored, "I guess."

With a slight clearing of her throat, Verna finally made a noise. Every head swiveled toward her. She drew her lips together like she was puckering up for a kiss and gave a quick lift of her chin toward Navvy. Was she pointing with her lips? Yes. She was definitely pointing with her lips.

The first words she spoke were so quiet we could hardly make them out. "I already know that is a Navajo horse."

I stared at her blankly. She lifted her chin. Yup, she was pointing with her lips again. She continued "...because of that brand."

She was right. There was a small brand on Navvy's right flank in the shape of a turtle. Horses from the reservation often carried a brand.

Dad whistled, "Well, you've got sharp eyes Verna, I'll say that for you."

A hot stab of jealousy went through my chest. "Sharp eyes" was one of my Dad's best compliments.

Verna didn't make a sound at supper, hiding behind her curtain of black hair and lifting her fork to her mouth with small, graceful motions. Her silence seemed to settle over the table, making everyone unnaturally quiet. Even Jimmy Scott didn't grunt while he chewed.

I brushed my teeth and changed into my nightgown in the bathroom, avoiding the inevitable coming embarrassment. When I came into my bedroom, Verna was unpacking. I got a book and sat against the headboard, pretending to read so I could watch her. She pulled a purple plastic case with a white handle out of the cardboard box, casually put it on the bed and snapped open the catch. The lid folded back like Dad's fishing tackle box and a mirror popped up. I couldn't help myself, and put down the book, crawling forward to see what was inside.

It was dazzling, a Maybelline treasure chest. There was a black bottle that looked like ink and said "liquid eyeliner" There were tweezers, a fluffy pink powder puff, a bottle of tan stuff to put on your face, green and blue eye shadow, White Shoulders perfume, a plastic bag of white cotton balls and a tube of midnight blue mascara.

Jealousy filled my heart. I sniffed, "Just so you know, my mom won't allow you to wear makeup. You're too young."

Verna calmly arranged her treasures, ignoring me. She continued unpacking the box and putting things away in the dresser. Suddenly she pulled out two blinding white cotton bras, folding each one neatly into the top drawer. I looked more closely at her chest. Holy Cow! Verna had bosoms.

Lately Willa and I had become obsessed with growing bosoms, an obsession that had so far not produced any results other than acute envy and frustration. We had made a pact to always say bosom, because breast was such an embarrassing word.

I tried to sound casual. "Where did you get those? I mean... those bras?"

Verna kept unpacking and folding, and finally said, "K-mart. Window Rock. These bras won't fit you" She paused, looking straight at me for the first time. "You are not even double A."

What in the heck was a double A? I decided to fake it. "Well, that's because I'm a... I'm a triple A."

"Ha!" Verna snorted scornfully. "Triple A is the worst size. I am already A-cup.

Embarrassment and anger made my face red and I blurted out the first thing that came to my mind. "Well, my mom has already ordered seven bras for me from the Sear's catalog—one for every day of the week—with bikini panties to match." I bounced out of bed and said. "They should be coming any day now." I slammed the door when I left the bedroom, but then opened it again and said, "Oh, and my cousin Willa is getting some too. She's my best friend". Slamming the door again I realized I was going to go straight to h-e-double toothpick for lying.

I found my mom stretched out on the couch in the living room, her blue glasses perched on the tip of her nose. She was reading a Reader's Digest Condensed Book.

Slumping glumly on the braided rug, I leaned against the couch. "Mom, this is not going to work out."

She took off her glasses and looked at me. Her voice was mild. "Oh?"

I scrambled, "She—Verna points with her lips Mom!" She raised an eyebrow.

I said "Well don't you think that is weird?" Mom sighed, rubbing at the bridge of her nose.

Stumbling on I said. "Verna can't even speak English and you should see the boatload of makeup she brought!"

Mom's voice snapped "Oh for heaven's sake. You go straight back to your bedroom young lady, and start being nice to that scared little girl. And I don't want to hear any more about it."

Angry, I hurled a desperate last shot. "What if she tries to kill me in the night while I'm sleeping? I suppose you wouldn't even care!"

Whirling around I stomped away, locking myself in the bathroom. I sat on the toilet and fumed. Willa and I had tried all summer to get our mothers to buy us training bras. Willa got the same answer from Aunt Holly that I got from my Mom, "For heaven's sake Effie, there's no need to rush. When you really need a bra I'll get you one. Quit trying to grow up so fast." Now Verna had moved in with her own set of bras *and* the bosoms to put in them. I yanked off a length of toilet paper and blew my nose. None of this was fair. This whole situation just kept getting worse.

When I opened my bedroom door the light was out and Verna was already in bed, her body a thin ridge under the quilt. I knelt by the bed and said my prayers, pleading with God to send her back where she came from. Climbing in, I slept on the edge, as far away as possible.

CHAPTER SEVEN

Milking with the Missies

The week passed with only a handful of words between me and Verna. I continued to change clothes in the bathroom, avoiding her whenever I could. I sat by Willa on the bus and tried to pretend Verna had nothing to do with me. Thank goodness she wasn't assigned to my class. School was a welcome break from being around her.

I had been responsible for feeding our horses and our milk cow, Bell since I was six. This chore wasn't really hard but it was annoyingly regular. Nothing made my Dad's neck get red faster than someone neglecting animals. Jimmy Scott and I had sat through plenty of flinty lectures on that subject. Now that Verna was here, I was glad for the excuse to get out of the house every morning. Mom had given her the baby job of setting the table for breakfast.

On Saturday morning, I was filling up the water troughs when Gussie and Lizzie came into the barn. Sheesh, it wasn't even seven o'clock yet.

I turned off the faucet. "What are you guys doing here?"

Gussie stuck out her chin. "It's a free country isn't it?" Every inch of the twins matched, from their wispy blonde hair down to their stubby toes. Willa's stout little sisters were her opposites. She had curly red hair and was as skinny as me. Neither Gussie nor Lizzie had front teeth at the moment, and they both had chapped red rings around their mouths from licking their lips.

Even though I was more than twice as old as them, Gussie and Lizzie showed me no respect. I admit they had been cute during the baby stage, but somewhere on the way to five it wore off. They had grown as cocky as Bandy Roosters and bossy.

Lizzie thrust out an empty egg carton. "We need some eggs."

Gussie chimed in, "Yeah, all ours exploded when Lizzie dropped the basket."

"Only because you made me run."

"I didn't make..."

I interrupted before the Missies launched into one of their never-ending arguments. "Okay, okay, but I'm not hunting them for you, I've got chores."

Mom was crazy about Gussie and Lizzie. After I was born she had four miscarriages and had longed for more children. When Aunt Holly had Augusta and Elizabeth, Mom practically moved into their house. She helped every day for weeks, changing diapers, giving baths, holding one baby while the other nursed, and then trading for another round. Mom cleaned and did more laundry at Willa's house than she did at ours for months. We soon quit using the twins long names and started calling them Gussie and Lizzie. Uncle Slab called them "the Missies" from the first because he couldn't tell them apart.

I got the pliers down off the nail in the saddle shed and clipped both strands of wire from a bale of sweet alfalfa hay. Folding the wire, I threw it into the barrel by the door. I divided a thick slice of hay from the bale and carried it over to Bell's manger. A bigger section was for the horse's, divided up so all four horses could get their share. I liked things to be even.

Jimmy Scott came into the barn and got the milking stool out of the saddle shed. It wasn't really a stool; just two short 2x4's nailed into a T-shape. He gave Gussie and Lizzie his usual welcome. "Who let you twerps out of your cage?

"You're the one who lives in a cage." Gussie jumped off a bale and dropped an egg. It bounced on the soft barn floor and didn't break.

"Yeah, you're...you're a stinky gorilla escaped from the zoo." Lizzie was madly in love with Jimmy Scott. "Can we watch you milk?"

Jimmy Scott grunted, "No because you'll make noise and scare Bell and she'll kick me."

"We won't, we won't! We'll be quiet." Lizzie shouted.

Jimmy Scott pushed on Bell's rump. "C'mon girl, move over." Bell took a small step and he settled on the milking stool. Our milk cow faithfully produced a calf every year, each one receiving a Bell-name; Bluebell, Bellpepper, Tinkerbell, Dumbbell, and Libertybell. Dad wanted to name one Hells Bells but Mom wouldn't let him.

Watching Jimmy Scott milk was one of my favorite things. I knew Bell would never really kick him, in spite of what he said to Lizzie. She barely had enough oomph to swish her tail at flies. Jimmy Scott wiped her bag off with a cloth and then settled the bucket nice and snug between his knees, tilting it forward a smidge. The first shots of milk hit the bottom of the milk pail with a tinny racket. Tiger and Otis, the barn cats came running and sat up expectantly. Jimmy Scott shot a squirt of milk at them that left them licking their whiskers with long pink tongues. Gussie and Lizzie laughed hysterically—everything their hero did was hilarious.

I was glad I didn't have to milk. I had never really learned how to do it well. I could make a thin trickle come out of a cow teat, but not a good stream. My plan was to never get good at it thanks to advice from mom. She told me that she had agreed to marry a rancher with the condition that she would never have to milk cows. I planned to be smart and sassy like my mom if I ever got married. I had already started forming my own list of conditions beginning with; "no toe-nail clipping in my presence." Every month or so Dad would laboriously pull off his socks and start operating away on his tough old toenails, carefully piling them up in a splintery mound. It gave me the shudders. Yup, I was definitely going to put my foot down about that one.

Jimmy Scott leaned the top of his head into Bell's side while he pulled down rhythmically. The sound muffled after an inch of milk was in the pail, and a layer of foam started building.

Gussie elbowed me. "I saw that Indian girl."

Lizzie chimed in. "Yeah, you guys are lucky, mom told me and Gussie we can't have a foster sister."

I said "Well, you can have Verna."

"Don't you like her?" The twins spoke in unison. I swear; each of them must have got half of the same brain. Their thoughts were always riding on the same train.

"Nope" I said firmly.

Again they chimed in together "Why not?"

I said "None of your beeswax. But I'll trade you Verna for Willa any day."

Gussie said, "Okay by us. Anybody's gotta be better than stinky old Willa."

I gave Gussie a little push. "Aren't you guys supposed to be taking those eggs home?"

Gussie's hand flew up to her mouth. "Yikes Lizzie, we better go."

They were already running out the barn door when I yelled, "Hey, wait... the eggs." I picked up the half-filled carton and held it out. Lizzie ran back and snatched it.

I said "Careful or you're gonna break..." It was useless; they were already hightailing it for home. Aunt Holly was going to end up with a carton full of scrambled eggs.

The milk bucket was almost full, each squirt sounded rich and satisfying.

I shooed away a fly. "Jimmy Scott, do you like Verna?" I desperately wanted Jimmy to be on my side.

He said "I dunno, I can hardly tell she's there. She's so quiet she's like a ghost."

"Yeah, and she's haunting me full time." I laughed but Jimmy didn't laugh along with me.

He finished and stood up, holding the full milk pail in one hand and the stool in the other.He said" Maybe you should try being nice to her."

My blood boiled and I could feel my face turning red. I turned around and stomped out of the barn and back to the house. How had Verna got everyone in our family on her side, including Jimmy Scott? All she did was give us all the silent treatment and hide behind her hair. I didn't get it. And I didn't have a friend in the world except Willa.

CHAPTER EIGHT

Finnegan's wake

I shouldn't have been surprised when Verna got to ditch church Sunday. Holy cow, Mom and Dad would ever let me get away with that. I was grateful to be gone from her for a while, but it was wrong that she didn't have to live by the same rules that I did. Besides, if anyone needed to go to church it was Verna. I had heard her tell my Mom that she had an uncle who was a medicine man. She definitely needed to learn about Jesus to set her straight.

After school on Monday Verna and I were eating a piece of warm bread and jam when the phone rang. It was Willa. "Effie, you have to get over here quick."

I mumbled through a mouthful of bread. "Why?"

Willa blurted out. "Finnegan's dead!"

I quit chewing. The bread didn't taste good anymore. Finnegan was famous, a big red Irish setter that belonged to the Caldwells, who were one set of our bazillion cousins. I couldn't remember a time when he hadn't been part of their family. At family get-togethers he was right in the middle of things. He sat placidly while he got jumped on, and let the babies yank his ears. I had ridden him like a horse until I turned four and Dad made me stop. He was a shaggy red babysitter. When Gussie was little, I remember watching as she mauled him for a while and then lost interest and started toddling off. Finnegan raised a paw and tried to corral her so she would come back and play some more. He was the friendliest dog ever born.

I twirled the phone cord round and round my hand as Willa went on. "He got hit by a car. You know how he couldn't hear anymore? He just wandered off the porch and into the road."

Losing Finnegan hit hard, a good dog was just below a good horse in my animal hierarchy. I felt my eyes tear up and water ran from my nose. "Are we going to have a funeral?"

"Of course we are." I could hear Willa blowing her nose. "Everyone's coming. Bring the wagon. And hurry."

Laying animals to rest with a prayer and song had been a tradition in life with my cousins. There was something grand about officiating at a final farewell that made us all feel important. But Finnegan dying, well this called for a funeral-*deluxe*.

I hung up the phone and ran to the living room, where mom was sewing a button on Dad's shirt. My words came out in a rush "Mom, Finnegan got hit by a car and he's dead and so we're going to have a funeral."

She pushed up her glasses. "That poor old dog. I wish that for once this family could have a pet that died of natural causes."

I was so impatient I bounced on my toes. "Can I go right now? They need the wagon and everybody's going to be there."

Mom snipped the thread with her scissors. "Sure, but take Verna with you. You can't go without her."

I whined with frustration. "Mo-om—this is an emergency."

She looked over the top of her glasses at me and her eyebrows went up.

I said "She probably won't even want to go."

"Well, I guess you better ask her then." She went back to her sewing.

With no time to argue I rushed into the kitchen, where Verna was sitting at the table taking dainty bites of bread and jam.

I blurted "Hey Verna, want to go to Willa's and help with Finnegan's funeral?"

She quit chewing. (Long Navajo pause.) "Who is Finnegan?"

My words tumbled over themselves "The Caldwell's dog—he got hit by the car. We're going to have the biggest funeral ever. C'mon, funerals are a blast."

"No." Her answer was curt. She put the bread down and pulled her lips over her teeth.

Frustrated I said, "Why not? All the cousins will be there. You can meet everybody you haven't met yet. We'll have songs and prayers and everything. It will be cool."

Verna shook her head and didn't look up.

Throwing my hands up I said "You don't have to do anything, you can just watch."

No answer.

Great. Here I was trying to be nice—give her a chance to get to know all the cousins and she wouldn't even go. "Verna…"

She interrupted "Navajos don't mess with the dead."

What in the heck was she talking about? Now I was ticked off. "We're not messing with the dead, we're burying a dog." Geez Louise what was wrong with this girl?

Verna just stared at her half eaten bread.

I said "You don't have to do anything. C'mon, Mom won't even let me go if you don't come." I hated that I was begging. "You can just stand there, I promise."

I fumed as I watched Verna lift the bread and take a minuscule bite. She chewed. "Okay, maybe when I finish." All her movements had a kind of smoothness to them that made me feel gawky. I couldn't take any more.

Turning around I yelled back over my shoulder, "I'll go and get the wagon and meet you out front" letting the screen door slam behind me. When Verna finally came out she trailed behind me as I pulled our big red radio flyer wagon up the road to Willa's house. What did Verna mean, *messing with the dead*? What did Navajos do when something died—just ignore it and pretend it didn't happen? I did not get her at all.

Willa's lawn was full of cousins and I soon forgot all about Verna. The Missies and the littlest cousins were tearing branches off the weeping willow tree. I directed them and we lined the wagon bed where they draped gracefully over the sides. Four of the big boys carried Finnegan to the prepared wagon, folding up his legs so all of him would fit inside. A lump came up in my throat at the sight of our lifeless companion, and for a moment or two my excitement ebbed. The crowd headed out east toward the stock pond, taking turns pulling the wagon through the fallow alfalfa field and over the bumpy road. When we finally got to the pond I was sweaty and thirsty and wishing I had brought something to drink. The stock pond water was low and murky and I quickly decided I wasn't quite that desperate.

We agreed on a good spot next to a juniper tree without too many rocks. Clay took charge because he was fourteen and born bossy. His blonde flattop haircut glistened in the late afternoon sunlight.

"Everybody take your hats off," he commanded. I looked around. No one was even wearing a hat. I rolled my eyes at Willa. At least ten yards away from the group, Verna stood by herself, looking off into the distance like she was the only person on earth.

"We are gathered here today to talk about what a great dog Finnegan was." Clay pitched his voice unnaturally deep. "First we would like to start with an invocation."

"What's that?" Lizzie wrinkled her nose suspiciously.

Willa gave her an elbow. "Shhh Lizzie, it's the opening prayer."

Clay took his time looking around, enjoying the power. "Max, you say it. Everybody, bow your heads." Oh shoot, Max said prayers that were longer than most church meetings.

In a fakey radio announcer voice, Max began. I decided to get comfortable and sank down to the ground cross-legged, bowed my head and closed my eyes. After what seemed like an hour

I couldn't stand it any longer. I opened my eyes and looked around. Max was the only one that still had his eyes scrunched closed as he droned on. The effort of sounding magnificent made him look constipated. I cracked Willa up by cutting my throat with my hand. Gussie tiptoed over in front of him and wiggled her fingers in her ears. This made Clay laugh and he hissed, "Okay man, wrap it up."

After a chorus of hearty amens, Clay announced the opening song and picked Willa to lead. She raised both arms. "Okay everybody, it's "Jesus wants Finnegan for a Sunbeam." Everyone tried to outdo each other, singing with gusto as Willa waved her knobby baton.

Jesus wants Finnegan for a sunbeam

To shine for him each day

In every way try to please him

At home, on the range, at play.

A sunbeam, a sunbeam

Jesus wants Finnegan for a sunbeam

A sunbeam, a sunbeam

Finnegan is a sunbeam for him.

Sunbeam was our go-to song because it could be adapted to any creature. Clay asked each of us to share our favorite memory. Cody went first and remembered that Finnegan never really had that stinky dog breath, and that he hadn't pooped on the lawn too much.

As the stories began, I looked at Willa. It was time for her to share her special talent of crying pretty much whenever she wanted to. I watched as she gave the bottom of her nose a little pinch, to make her eyes water and get things rolling. The next step in her technique was to think about something really sad— like getting no Christmas presents or being forced to eat split pea soup. Once the tears started, it was like real sadness took over the fake sadness, really quite miraculous. Willa's eyes filled up and she gave a sharp little sob to set the mood.

Rachael twisted her long braid and described in a quavering voice how Finnegan had been really great at rounding up milk cows. Soon she was totally carried away with a big whopper about how Finnegan killed a rattlesnake that was about to strike a baby. It was out of control from then on as one cousin after another took their turn. Finnegan got credit for saving drowning calves, chasing away robbers and peeing out a forest fire. After a half hour of this we were all worked up. Willa wasn't the only one crying.

Every story seemed so real. I could imagine Finnegan doing all of it. I knew he could have done all of it. Emotion swirled around us like smoke, filling us, draining us. It was powerful. I wiped my eyes and caught sight of Verna, away from the group, still staring over the stock pond. Was her heart made of stone?

Heidi started singing. "Swing low, sweet chariot, coming to take Finnegan home, swing low, sweet chariot comin' to take Finnegan home." This was the only part of the song that she knew and so she sang the lines over and over and we all joined in. Willa grabbed my hand, I grabbed Gussie's and eventually we were joined in a big grieving circle around the red wagon, where Finnegan lay on wilted willow branches.

After I said a short closing prayer we took turns with the three shovels we had brought and dug the grave. It was a good spot—pretty easy shoveling, and there were only a couple rocks to pry out. We put Finnegan in the hole and everyone pitched in to cover him with the red dirt until there was a nice smooth mound. Suzy volunteered to go home and make a cross that we could bring back later for a marker. For now, we piled some rocks on top.

We all sat around the grave, exhausted. We had never thrown a better funeral. How could anything ever top this.

Then Clay stood up, dusting off his jeans, "Hey guys I have an idea."

Every head turned toward him.

"Let's dig Finnegan up, and take him back home. Then to-morrow we can all meet again, haul him back and have another funeral!"

Willa and I looked at each other, breaking in to big grins. That Clay, he was some kind of genius. I hoped I was that smart by the time I was fourteen. What amazing leadership.

"Wait, where are we going to store him?" I looked around, hating to spoil anything.

"How about my cellar?" Willa volunteered. "It's nice and cool and no one will find him there."

"Yeah, because if we leave him out a coyote might smell him..."Rachael said, "or a mountain lion."

"There aren't any mountain lions around here," Clay sounded disgusted.

"Are too." Lizzie broke in, " Gussie and I saw six of them in our cottonwood tree. Didn't we, Gussie?" Gussie nodded her head vigorously. The Missies always backed each other up.

"Okay, okay," Clay said, ignoring the Missies highly suspect wild animal sighting. "The cellar will work. Everybody help dig him up."

Finnegan looked quite a bit worse for wear after we un-earthed him. His beautiful red coat was dusty and I tried not to look at his face, which was starting to look scary, especially where his mouth pulled back from his teeth and his tongue hung out.

Verna trailed a good distance behind the group as we pulled the wagon back as fast as we could, stopping before we got too close to Willa's house. Willa snuck in and came out with an old green army blanket and we wrapped Finnegan up. The wimpy cousins took off, leaving Clay, Willa and I to wrestle Finnegan down the cellar stairs. We hid him as best we could, laying him against the shelves in back of some buckets of wheat.

When I came outside, I found that Verna had already left, leaving me to pull the wagon home alone. Dang, I was really going to be late for supper.

We were all at the table eating when the phone rang. Mom answered it.

"Oh hi, Holly." Her eyebrows went together and she listened for a long time. "You have got to be kidding" she said as she turned around and stared right at me. I felt my heart start to beat faster. Uh oh, Aunt Holly must have found out Finnegan had returned from the dead.

Mom's voice was rising, "I can't believe…. I bet it scared you silly. I swear I don't what these kids are thinking sometimes. So shall I…. Yes, I'll send her right away."

She hung up the phone and turned around, folding her arms. Her mouth stretched into a line and and her eyes drilled through me. I put down my fork.

"What was that all about Lila?" Dad asked.

Mom answered Dad, but didn't take her eyes off me. "Willa and Effie organized a funeral for Finnegan today."

"Aren't they always having a funeral for something or other?" Dad took a big bite of bread.

"I guess this one was really a lot of fun," Mom put her hands on her hips. "Wasn't it Effie?"

I spoke quickly "It wasn't just me and Willa, all the cousins were there…and Verna too." I glanced at Verna, who had finally lifted her head up, looking interested.

Mom threw her hands in the air, her voice rising incredulously. "It was *so* much fun that they dug that poor dog up again and put him in Holly's cellar so they could have *another* funeral tomorrow!"

Dad started laughing. This was good. One mad parent was far less dangerous than two. He laughed and laughed, pushing back from the table and taking his handkerchief out of his back pocket to he could wipe his eyes.

"James," Mom's voice was icy "you wouldn't think it was so darn funny if you knew how much it scared Holly. She went down in the cellar to get some peaches and saw a big lump in the corner covered with a blanket. When she pulled up a corner to see what it was, there was that poor old dog grinning up at her. It almost scared her to death."

This made Dad laugh even harder. I glanced at Jimmy Scott, who gave me a superior big brother look and shaking his head with pity at my. Verna looked at me like I smelled bad and gave a little scoot away from me on the bench.

Mom took a step toward me and shook her finger at me. "Effie, you hotfoot it right back to Willa's, and take your wagon. You kids are going to bury that poor dog right now, tonight. You are definitely not going to leave him in Holly's cellar until tomorrow afternoon. Of all the harebrained ideas you kids have ever come up with...."

I was already on my feet, heading for the back door, grabbing a flashlight on my way out. This burial was not going to be near as fun as the first one.

When I finally crawled into bed it was after ten o'clock.I hurt all over with tiredness. I was relieved that Verna was asleep. I definitely didn't want to hear her say I told you so. I started drifting off when I heard her speak.

Her voice was low "You shouldn't have done that."

"What are you talking about?" I was wide awake again.

"Digging up that dog." The words were calm and slow. It gave me the creeps.

She brought her hand out of the covers and laid her arm across her forehead. "Now something bad is going to happen."

A chill went down my neck and I pulled the quilt up around my ears.

"Navajo's understand, but you people..." she didn't finish.

I pulled the quilt tighter, stealing some of Verna's covers. "Us people? Do you mean—us white people?"

"You shouldn't have done that." She turned her back to me.

I couldn't sleep for a long time.

CHAPTER NINE

Happy birthday to Jill

"Verna's not even invited Mom. We can't just show up with an extra person." Half my life was negotiating with my Mom about Verna. I was her real kid. Couldn't she see how hard this all was? My mom's affection had sometimes been a little hard to come by, but lately it was completely gone.

Mom said "I'll call Jill's Mom, I'm sure Sheila won't mind."

I was horrified. "Mo-o-o-m." There was that annoying mouse squeak I couldn't seem to control. "You can't you just can't."

Willa and I had been counting down the days until Jill's birthday party. Jill had been queen of every grade since kindergarten. Willa and I were scared of her in a thrilling and worshipful way. She lived in town, shaved her legs, and all her clothes matched. She didn't even call them clothes, she called them "outfits". Jill did her shopping in Phoenix and scorned the Sears catalog that Willa and I loved. She flashed with hardware—hoops in her pierced ears and braces on her teeth. She got her hair done at the New U before picture day every year and her nails were painted not chewed. Jill was the most popular girl in our class and now Willa and I had been invited to her first boy/girl party. Mom was going to ruin it completely by making me bring Verna.

"I don't think Navajos believe in parties Mom." Maybe she would think I knew something about Navajo traditions.

"Where in the world did you get that idea?" Mom shook out a towel with a sharp snap.

I tried another tack. "She doesn't have a swimsuit."

Mom said "Well, since you have a new one, she can borrow your old one."

I was horrified "Trust me, she won't want to do that. It's unhumane."

"Unhumane?" Now she was laughing at me.

"You know, germy. She won't want my cooties from down there." I gestured vaguely. Mom snapped another towel, stiff from being dried outside on the clothesline. "I think you mean "unhygienic", and I'm sure I could easily get rid of your cooties in my next batch of laundry." A cupboard door slammed around the corner in the kitchen.

Mom gave me a glare and called out, "Verna, is that you?"

Dang that girl was sneaky. I was used to people that clomped around so you could tell where they were. Verna just appeared like Caspar the ghost.

"I don't want to go to that party." Verna said.

My face was hot with embarrassment and I mumbled "A... well. I could..."

Verna gave me a disdainful look and turned her back on me. As she left the room she said. "I don't like swimming."

I was flooded with relief (Thank you God!) that my first boy/girl party was not going to be ruined by my weird foster sister. I had enough to worry about.

Willa and I loved swimming, especially since we were finally old enough to go to the community pool without a parent. We went almost every week and once in a great while we could talk Jimmy Scott into going with us. If there were older girls around to see his muscles, he would pick me up right out of the water, lift me overhead and throw me. Then he would do the same for Willa. It was a blast, being launched through the air and landing with a huge splash. He also did crazy dives and tricks off of the diving board.

Jill's parents had rented the whole pool just for the party, another sign of their enormous wealth. The plan was to swim for an hour and then gather at Jill's house for hamburgers, cake and ice cream.

I held up the towel for Willa while she changed in the stall that had no door and then she did the same for me. The cement was clammy under our bare feet, giving me goosebumps. I felt giddy with excitement and nerves. I happily pulled on my new swimsuit, which was bright pink with wavy white lines. I had grown a couple inches and had been tugging my ratty old suit out of my bum for 6 months. When I found a cute two piece in the catalog Mom said "Why I bet I can make that Effie!" That's what she said about everything that cost too much. Except for my jeans, Mom had sewed most all of my clothes since I was born. I'd had my doubts about the swimsuit project, but it had really turned out cute.

When I came out of the stall Willa said, "Gosh Effie, that is sooo darling!"

"Thanks, I like it too." I admired myself in the cloudy mirror.

We left our towels and our change of clothes in a stack on the bench, carefully hiding our underwear, and hurried out of the dressing room. The smell of chlorine and echoing voices hit us as we turned the corner. Scads of boys and girls were already splashing in the shallow end batting a beach ball around.

Willa and I stood watching for a second, huddling together with our arms wrapped around our stomachs, hands holding our elbows. A boy-girl party, this was really big. I was flooded with the relief of having a best friend to lean on. It would have been way too scary alone.

Willa elbowed me, "Do you want to do the diving board first?"

"Yeah, let's do it." As I walked self consciously on the rough cement deck I wondered if any boys were looking at me in my new suit. Did I really look good in it?

Willa climbed up on the diving board first and yelled, "Watch this!" over her shoulder at me. She ran to the end and bounced hard again and again. The bouncing board echoed so loudly that everyone in the shallow end turned to watch her. She sprang high into the air, spreading her arms and legs out wide. It looked like she was going to do a gigantic belly flop but at the last possible moment she tucked and did a cannonball. A fountain splashed toward the roof high above. A cheer went up.

Willa surfaced with a gasp and started for the side. I yelled, "Oh yeah, well watch this!" Running to the end of the board, I took one high bounce and then did a perfect fish flip. This was my specialty, and had taken a lot of practice. I stretched out, arms above my head and didn't tuck my body at all, but flipped completely around once and went in feet first.

I hit the water hard and immediately knew I was in big trouble. As I plummeted for the bottom with the force of my entry, the top of my swimsuit stripped completely off over my head and arms. I reached out to grab it as it began to sink in front of my face. Kicking toward the surface, the bottom half of the suit slipped down to my ankles. I was just able to snag it with my big toe before it sank to the bottom of the pool. Writhing, I tried to get my feet back through the leg holes as I came up for air. When I broke through, I was holding onto the waistband of the bottom half with one hand and the top in front of me with the other hand. I wanted to plunge right back to the bottom of the pool to put it all back on, but I had to get a breath.

I blinked water out of my eyes. The kids were all coming toward the deep end! Dog paddling frantically, I stuck my head through my top, trying to stay above water while I pulled it back on. Both pieces of my swim suit felt gigantic and heavy. I got my arms and head back through, but the suit had stretched so much when it got wet, that both armholes and neckline sagged almost to my waist. Just barely holding onto the bottom half, I knew I could not keep everything together and stay afloat at the same time.

Joey, the cutest boy in my class was on the diving board,

yelling down at me as I struggled in the water. I splashed desperately, hoping he wouldn't be able to tell what was happening.

"Hey Effie, get out of the way." Joey yelled through cupped hands. Good grief, at least he was blind without his glasses. My mind raced. Either I was going to drown holding on to my suit or have to swim away without it. How in the heck could I make it to the side and not be completely naked when I got there? I called out weakly to Willa but either she didn't hear me or ignored me as she got back in line behind the diving board.

Grabbing a handful of soggy material at my waist I paddled awkwardly to the side. By now, everyone was lined up at the diving board waiting a turn to show off. Holding on to the side of the pool I inched my way slowly to the shallow end, trying to look casual. Thank goodness it was empty with everyone in line at the diving board. Finally reaching the farthest corner I was able to lean my back against it and adjust the suit, pulling it up to cover me. I pinned it tightly in place with my arms clenched to my sides. I was completely pooped.

I wondered if I could I climb out but knew there was no chance. I would never make it to the dressing room without showing my bare hiney.

The longest hour of my life passed as I used every muscle to keep my suit on. Willa had abandoned me and was having the time of her life. Once in a while someone would swim over and ask why I wasn't playing games or diving. I would say casually, "I'm just resting" or "Maybe later." When a volley ball was thrown my direction, I couldn't even reach out to catch it. I had to pretend like I didn't see it, while it smacked me on the side of the head.

When Jill's mom finally announced that it was time to get out and go have hamburgers, I was so relieved tears came to my eyes. I was worn out from struggling to keep my suit up with my tightly clenched arms and from trying to look natural. Everyone finally cleared out and headed to the dressing room—including Willa. What in the heck was I supposed to do now? Was I going to be stuck in here forever while my best friend went off to the party? I was steaming as I gathered the sodden folds of my cursed swim suit around my shivering body, climbing laboriously out of the pool. Jill's mom passed me as I hurried into the dressing room. She sounded annoyed." Hurry up Effie or we'll all be waiting on you."

When I got to the dressing room I snatched my towel, wrapping it tightly around me and grabbed my pile of clothes. I went into a toilet stall, locking it. As I unwrapped my towel, the hideous pink mass dropped, thudding to the floor with a thwap like a dead seal. I must have been wearing five gallons of pool water. Dressing in a hurry, I wrapped the suit in my towel, and carried my heavy load out to the waiting car.

Jimmy Scott picked me up after I called home, so I could leave the party early. I stomped into the kitchen where Mom was peeling potatoes. She said, without turning around from the sink, "Oh, hi honey. How was the swimming party?"

When I didn't answer she looked over her shoulder. I let my towel unroll and her horrible creation fell to the linoleum with a thud.

She bent and picked up both pieces. "What in the world?" Her voice trailed off as she felt the weighty blobs that had once been my beautiful swimming suit.

Mom said "Oh, Effie. Oh no—I can't believe—I should have tested this fabric in the water before… Oh my, this fabric certainly is absorbent isn't it?"

I began to wail and she took me into her arms. "Honey, I am *so* sorry. You know, don't you, that I certainly didn't mean for this to happen. Did anyone notice? Tell me all about it."

Through my wails I said "I did a flip off the board and it exploded. It got gigantic Mom! I couldn't even keep it on. Everyone in the whole world almost saw me bare-naked. I had to stay in the corner of the pool the whole time—and Willa just ditched me." I wiped both hands across my streaming eyes. "At Jill's house everybody kept asking me what was wrong with me. I had to pretend I had a stomachache and so I couldn't even eat Jill's birthday cake. It was the worst day of my whole life."

Mom led me to the couch and we sat down. I leaned into her, sobbing as she held me. "I guess I'll give up on sewing swimsuits," she said.

"And Willa just left me." I hiccuped.

Mom said "Oh Effie, I'm sure she didn't mean to."

With a shuddering breath I said "You can give this swimsuit to Willa's fat old Aunt Alberta. It's her size now."

Mom finally dared to laugh, wiping my eyes on her apron. She said "You know Effie, someday this will be a very funny memory. You really will look back on it and laugh."

"I will never ever ever laugh about this." I sniffed. "Mom, you've got to promise to never tell anyone."

She said "Of course I won't, don't worry about that. This is just between us girls. C'mon, I bet you are completely starved." She stood up and held her hand out to me. "How about some peanut butter honey on toast?"

The thought of peanut butter honey started to cheer me up until Verna came around the corner. Instead of avoiding my eyes she looked straight at me and the unusually cheerful look on her face told me she had been spying again and knew everything. That cheered me right back down again.

CHAPTER TEN

The canyon

Crawling out of a dream, it took a minute for my heart to slow. I had been trying to run through a sandy wash to keep up with Willa, but my legs wouldn't move, they kept sinking into the sand, too heavy and paralyzed. Poking my head out of the covers, the dim light coming in my window told me it was still early. Closing my eyes again I lay listening. Nope, dad wasn't up yet—no nose blowing honks in the bathroom.

I started when I felt movement in my bed. I still wasn't used to sleeping with someone. Looking over at the slight shape of Verna filled me once again with annoyance.

The night had not erased my angry feelings toward Willa. I had been betrayed by my only ally. I needed to have it out with Willa—explain how awful and stupid I felt huddling for an hour in the corner of the pool. Suddenly it came to me what I should do. We both needed to hike down the canyon. Talking there, un-interrupted, I was sure I could make her understand. The Canyon was a place we both loved.

Gathering my clothes, I eased the door open, tiptoed down the hall to the bathroom, peed and got dressed.

I made two cheese sandwiches, and went to the sink to fill my canteen. If I left a note, it might get me a couple free hours. "Mom" I wrote, "*Willa and I are going on a little hike. I'll do my chores after lunch. Promise, Effie.*"

As I slipped out the back door I felt so relieved. The early morning October air was chilly, under a cloudless sky. and I ran all the way to Willa's house. Dang it! Uncle Slab was on the front porch, a cigarette hanging underneath his mustache as he had the first smoke of the day. My uncle was as intimidating as Aunt Holly was nice. Even though he smoked Camels, he looked like the Marlboro man, tan and wrinkly—broken in like a good saddle. His skinny frame bent over a little at the shoulders under his light blue denim shirt. Dark red hair was slicked back on his head in Brylcreemed waves, which were perennially dented from his cowboy hat.

He squinted at me as I approached, making me feel uncomfortable, although I didn't know what about.

"Hi Uncle Slab." I said, "Is she awake, I mean, is Willa up yet?"

Two streams of smoke streamed out his thin nostrils, a warm, not unpleasant smell in the fall air. He said "Where's the fire?"

"We're not going to build a fire, uh, I mean, there's not a fire. I just wanted to see if Willa wanted to go to the canyon." I said.

The cigarette fell to the porch and was crushed under the worn toe of Uncle Slab's boot. He said "Canyon huh? I better not catch you girls digging in that Indian ruin over there."

Most people I knew thought that digging Indian ruins was a dandy hobby, but not Uncle Slab. He called people who collected pots and arrowheads "grave robbers". It was one rare subject he got talkative about. I held up my sack lunch "No, I just wanted to go on a little hike."

He said, "Well I suspect you'll have to roust Willa. Nobody else is awake yet." He turned away and I slipped past him into the dim house.

The bedroom door was open and the light was rosy coming through Willa's ruffled pink curtains. Fast asleep, head thrown back and her mouth open, her curly hair was a fuzzy red halo on the pillow. She woke immediately when I shook her shoulder, rubbing the sleep from her eyes. When I told her my plan to hike the canyon she got dressed in a flash. Willa recognized the narrow window of escape before being trapped by a mother with a chore list.

Heading east toward the canyon, we crossed a pasture of grass faded by cold nights and stopped at the barbed wire fence clogged with tumbleweeds. Willa held the wires apart so I could squeeze through and I returned the favor.

My favorite part of the canyon was here at the mouth, where narrow canyon walls flared out and sloped down gradually like an invitation. The deeper you went downstream, the higher the rocky walls climbed, forming a zigzagging passage for a little creek. Silver Creek must have been named by a salesman, because the water was the furthest thing from silvery. It varied from light muddy to dark muddy, depending on the season.

The canyon narrowed as we hiked with sections choked with coyote willows growing from both sides of the creek bank to the canyon wall. These willows weren't really trees—more like whips growing up from the ground with feathery green stuff on the end. It was hard to get through without getting snapped in the face. I felt tense, rehearsing in my mind how to talk to Willa. In all the years we had been friends, we had rarely fought. In fact I couldn't remember the last time I had been mad at her.

We stopped for a breather, sharing a drink from the canteen. After a good gulp she said, "Now, Effie, I want you to tell me something honestly."

"Tell you what honestly?" I was thrown. I was the one who needed to hash things out with Willa. What was she talking about?

Willa said "Promise you'll be completely honest?"

I frowned at her. "Are you saying I'm usually a liar?"

She shrugged, impatient. "C'mon, seriously. This is important."

"I'm not going to promise unless I know what I'm promising." I said, feeling obstinate.

"Effie, you know you can trust me." Willa sounded hurt.

I burst out "Oh really, like last night at the pool party?"

Willa swatted a bug away from her face and frowned. "What are you talking about? Effie, you're the one that just sat in the corner the whole time. Why were you being so stuck up?"

I spluttered "Are you kidding Willa? How can you even..." I lost it. The unfairness of Willa's judgment and every moment of the long humiliating night came flooding back. I pushed past her, flailing through the willows until I was in the clear, stumbling over the rough ground and trying to get away. Willa was yelling "Wait, Effie, just wait will ya?"

I ignored her and kept going, realizing suddenly that Picture Rock was above me, high up the canyon wall. I began climbing, stretching my legs and feeling the pull in my arms as I reached up for handholds. I could hear Willa behind me sputtering. "What in the heck! C'mon, Effie! Slow down!"

Climbing was one of the few things that I was better at than Willa. I had a wiry strength that made me what my dad called "a real mountain goat". I got to the top and hoisted myself up, winded.

Panting, Willa followed a minute later, lying on her belly after she had climbed up on the flat surface. The canyon floor lay far below us, 150 feet or so. With a bit of imagination, Silver Creek did have a slightly silvery sheen as it snaked its way downstream.

Directly in front of us, I could see my house off in the distance. Beyond it, about two miles away, the tall bare cottonwood trees at the edge of town looked pretty and peaceful. Willa's home was hidden by a little rise to the right. If I shaded my eyes, I could see Dad and Uncle Slab's alfalfa fields and fenced pasture. The view was beautiful and took in everything I loved best in the world.

Picture Rock was famous in our corner of northern Arizona. There were dozens of rocks with Indian writing in the canyon, but this was the most spectacular.

A large flat rock formed a floor, almost horizontal, jutting out like a shelf, with room enough for several people to sit on. At the back, against the canyon wall, there were two tall rocks that fit together as perfectly as a corner in a room. The surface of the sandstone was almost black, and most of the chiseled pictures on it were still distinct.

Willa and I had been here so many times we knew every figure by heart. Reaching out my finger, I traced the animal with antlers. I figured it must be an antelope because there were still lots of them on our range. There was a trail of tiny human footprints going from one side of the rock, to the corner and off to the other side. Beside the human footprints ran the footprints of an antelope. A person with long snake-like arms that ended with huge hands stretched across a corner. Geometric shapes were scattered here and there, some in clusters. My favorite carving in the black rock was a figure shaped like a woman, holding a baby in her arms, with a stick figure child by her side. More than once Willa and I had brought paper and pencils and done rubbings, the ancient pictures appearing magically from the stone under our pencils. There were also some more current carvings, including one that said "Ferdinand '23". Dad said this was probably made by one of the Basque sheepherders that brought huge herds through our land on their way to Phoenix for the winter.

Willa was still breathing hard when she said, "Now, are you gonna tell me what's going on or not Effie?" I tried not to, but started crying, sobbing out the whole humiliating story of the blobby swimming suit and the horrible ordeal. I said through my tears "And you didn't even care Willa! You were having such much fun, you were so—so popular."

Willa scooched over close, putting her arm around my shoulder, her words tumbling against my neck. "I am so sorry Effie. I really am. That is so rotten. Oh my gosh! Your suit really fell all the way off?" She started to laugh and then looked at me and made a futile attempt to choke it off. I giggled too, and lifted my t-shirt to wipe at my nose. "You really did ditch me Willa. You treated me like poop. I should hate you forever."

She said "But you won't, right?" Easing her hug, she kept her arm draped companionably around my shoulder. "Are you still mad Effie? I'll make it up to you, you know I will."

The sun felt warm on my head and my heart had warmed up too. "Naw, I'm not mad more. It's just that with Verna there ruining everything at home, I really need you." We sat quietly, relief that the familiar easy balance between us was restored. A crow squawked and then glided overhead, catching a draft of wind.

Willa's eyes sparkled, "Okay, now I have something really important to talk to you about." She took a deep breath "In your *completely* honest opinion—between us two, who do you think is going to be the first one to get kissed?"

I had to think for a minute, bewildered at this change of direction. "Sick, Willa, I don't even want to be kissed." I looked at her face to see if she was really serious about this. "It'll be you since you're the one thinking about it."

Willa said "I'm not really thinking about it, it's just that next year we are going to be in Junior High and there are going to be parties where they play kissing games..."

I leaned over a traced a chiseled footprint with my finger. This subject made me feel queasy.

I said "Who told you about the kissing games?"

Willa said "Jill."

This made sense. Jill was so pretty and popular, she had probably already been to scads of Junior High parties. I said" Jill has probably already kissed someone."

Willa scrunched her eyes shut and let out a dramatic breath. "I promised I wouldn't tell anyone this, but I have to tell you because you are my best friend and anyways, everyone knows I always tell you everything."

That was the way it was. We told each other everything. We

knew things about each other that no one in the world knew, including our Mom's. It was Willa's absolute duty to break her promise to Jill in order to fulfill a more important obligation to me as best friend.

"Tell me," I said.

Willa continued, her voice bright with excitement "You know how we were doing that game when everyone was diving for quarters?"

Glumly I said "You mean, everyone but me."

Willa said "Well, I saw Jill and Lewis kind of go off by themselves toward the deep end."

Ooo, this was getting interesting.

Willa's voice pitched higher with each word "I saw them dive down to the bottom and...."

She paused. She had a huge grin on her face, her blue eyes huge, her wild red hair on fire with sunlight, her bony knees poking through the holes in her jeans. Willa's hands went to her mouth, fingers to lips, ready to let the secret spill out.

I was impatient "So what happened? They dove to the bottom and...."

"They kissed!" she said triumphantly.

I said."Holy cow. Did you actually see them?" This was big.

Willa said "Oh yeah, I saw the whooole thing. They kissed all right. No doubt about it. It lasted for a while."

"Who started it?" I asked.

Willa said "Well, probably Lewis, you know what he's like. But Jill put her arms around him and seriously, she was kissing him back."

I was picturing it all in my mind; the dive to the bottom through eye-stinging chlorine water, the muffled sounds, the arms going out—around— pulling in—lips touching.

My words burst out "Gross! Little kids pee in that pool!"

We grabbed each other and fell back laughing on the warm rock. We laughed ourselves silly, egging each other on with choked out words.

"Oh Lewis…(wheezing laughter) I thought you were Charlie Tuna."

"Kiss me again Lewis (drawn out smooching sounds). I love your blubbery lips."

Tears were leaking out my eyes like they always did when I laughed too hard. I said "So Jill knew you saw her and made you promise not to tell?"

Willa said "Yeah, she was paranoid her Mom would find out."

I sat up, wiping at my eyes with the back of my hand. "It will probably be you who gets kissed first, Willa."

Willa's voice was sincere. "Naw, I think it will be you. Seriously, Effie, I think a lot of boys like you."

We lay back on the rock again, and I felt warmed by the sun on my face and by the friendship that always assumed the best about me. I was so relieved not to be mad at Willa anymore.

CHAPTER ELEVEN

The fall

Willa stood up and put out her hand, pulling me to my feet. "I know what we can do next…let's play like this is our stage. Let's have a performance." She faced the canyon sweeping both arms out dramatically. "…and this is the biggest arena in the whole world. We can take turns being the singer."

Already jittery with excitement, Willa turned around "Quick, find me a microphone." When Willa was enthused about something she turned bossy.

Climbing the short distance from the side of picture rock, I clambered over the top of the canyon wall. At the base of the twisty trunk of an old juniper was a piece of dried branch that would be perfect except it was too long. "I got one" I yelled down at Willa. "Just a minute, I gotta 'fix it." Laying the branch on a rock I stomped on it, the end cracking off under my tennis shoe. The part that was left almost looked like a microphone with a little knot at the top and a handle about a foot long.

Climbing back down I handed it to Willa. She looked it over. "Perfect." I sat down, my arms hugging my knees. This was going to be fun.

Turning, Willa faced the wide expanse in front of picture rock. Closing her eyes, she dropped her chin to her chest, raising her head slowly and dramatically, until her chin was high. Lifting the microphone to her mouth with one hand, she flipped her other hand out as her throaty voice belted through the clear air:

"Born free, as free as the wind blows

As free as your wart grows

Born free to let out a fart."

I burst out laughing. This was one of Willa's special talents. She could take any song and on the spot change all the words around so that they were hilarious. I often tried my hand at this, but wasn't good at coming up with funny rhymes.

"Live free, and beauty surrounds you

Until someone pounds you

And sends you to live on a star."

Willa kept singing, each line crazier than the last until she ended with a big finish.

"Live free and lice are for giving

And life is worth living

CAUSE—YOU'RE—BORN—FREE!" Willa stretched each word to a sensational climax. As the last note faded, she bent from the waist, flopping her head and arms down like a rag doll, then rose up to bow again and again.

"Thank ya, thank ya verra much." It was her best Elvis.

I was clapping hard and laughing so much that tears were coming out of my eyes again when Willa sank down beside me. She loved to make me laugh. It was one of the reasons we got along so well. She needed an audience and I thought she was the funniest person in the world.

"Do another one," I said. "It sounds so cool when you sing really loud and slow because it echoes. Listen." I grabbed the stick microphone out of her hand and stood up. Turning around, I faced the canyon and with my feet apart. I sang as loudly as I could, waving my free arm like Willa had done. "'Cause... you're... born... free...!"

The sounds bounced back, soft echoes mingling the words. Backing up a step I took a giant bow.

Willa sprang up—all excited again. She stepped in front of me, her back to the canyon "Wait Effie, let me have the microphone back, I have another song to sing." I was laughing so hard it hurt, bent over and holding my stomach.

"Effie, let me see it." Willa was laughing as she lunged toward me, trying to pull the microphone out of my hand.

I pulled my hand back "No, wait a second, I'm not done…" I held the microphone at my chest but Willa grabbed hold of it too. She gave a little yank and it came free from my hand, but suddenly she was staggering backwards. At the same time I struggled to keep my balance falling forward on my knees.

Willa was so excited, thinking only about her next performance when she dropped backwards off the stage into nothing.

I heard a short scream and then it was gone and I didn't see what knocked the sound from her throat. By the time I scrambled to the edge and looked over she had already hit once and was falling again. There were no more screams, just faint thuds, followed by puffs of dust. I don't know how many times she hit and fell and hit and fell again, but when she finally stopped it felt like I had been watching her for hours.

I scooted backward like a crab, as far away from the edge as I could. Nothing felt safe anymore. Pressing my back against the stone I closed my eyes and screamed, "Willa! Willa! Answer me Willa!" My voice was horrible in my ears. There was no answer. My teeth started to chatter and my body went stiff and cold.

What do I do? I did not know what to do. My mind would not work, freezing up like my body. I couldn't think straight. I felt a magnet pulling me, tugging me over the edge of Picture Rock, to follow Willa. I was too scared to move.

I shut my eyes, but that made my head whirl around so I opened them again. The sun was so bright! I tried to think clearly, tried talking to myself. *I have to go down to her now. I need to go down to her. I want to help Willa.* Panic kept my arms and legs from moving. They would not work. "I have to go. I have to go."

Repeating it, talking aloud to myself. I finally was able to get my legs to move while I told myself, *Willa is waiting for me.*

I climbed carefully off the ledge of Picture Rock and made my way down the canyon wall by inching slowing on my bum. Too afraid to stand, I could only to look a few feet in front of me at a time, even though I had climbed up and down this trail hundreds of times before. My body was shaking and clumsy, my arms and legs rubbery and weak. I went so slowly, it seemed to take forever.

I could see Willa now. She was about halfway down to the bottom and was lying in front of a small juniper. Steadily I inched my way down. It was so hard! How had I climbed in this canyon so many times without falling? It seemed impossible now.

Lying on her side, one of Willa's arms was flung over her face like she was shading her eyes. Her hair was dull with dust and and there were slide marks in the red dirt where she had slid against the tree. Her jeans were coated dust.

Now that I was with my friend, a calm feeling suddenly flowed like warm water through my veins. My arms and legs seemed to thaw.

"Willa," I said gently, like I was waking her from a nap.

"Willa." I shook her shoulder a little, reached out and picked up her wrist, moving her arm away from her head to lie across her chest. Her red curls covered her face and I moved them aside. Her eyes were open, looking at nothing. She looked fine; she didn't even look scared. She was just—still.

She was dead. I don't really know how I knew it. Except—that if she were alive she would have been calling for me.

Willa would have been calling my name.

I left her then and ran home. The only thing I remember about that mile is that my feet seemed to only skim the ground. I had the speed and strength of a yearling colt. Every step was sure and I could have kept running until morning.

When I found my mother, I still held the microphone in my hand.

CHAPTER TWELVE

Babes in the woods

It was very late. The sheriff, Tot Crandell and his men were long gone and finally the crowd of relatives and friends went home too. I peeled off my jeans and took a long bath, washing away the red dirt. Sitting in the bathtub, I cried but no tears came out, my crying reservoir was empty. Wrapping my hair in a towel I looked in the mirror My face looked fat and splotchy.

After I put my nightgown on, Mom knelt beside me while I cried my way through my short prayer and then sat beside me on the bed, smoothing back my wet hair and tracing my eyebrows, the line of my nose, my lips and cheekbones lightly with her finger, like she used to do when I was little and I lay my head in her lap at church.

"Where's Verna?" I asked. It was the first time I'd thought of my foster sister all day.

Mom said "She fell asleep on the couch so I just covered her up with a blanket. She'll be fine there for tonight."

It was such a relief to think that I wouldn't have to sleep with Verna that I finally began to relax, loving the feeling of my mother's cool fingers on my skin.

"Do you want to talk some more about today, Effie?" my Mom's voice was gentle.

"I dunno," I could feel myself tensing again. I lay there, not speaking for a few minutes. I didn't want to talk about it. I had not been able to tell anyone about that last moment

—when I yanked back my hand and Willa didn't let go. The story I had sobbed out first to my Mom, and then many more times throughout the day was that Willa accidentally lost her balance and fell backwards. There had been no further probing questions. Everyone had treated me with delicate kindness, even gruff old Tot Crandell. As I answered his questions I concentrated on his ample belly that strained against the pearl snaps of his khaki uniform. The guilt I felt about Willa's fall stayed burning inside me, waiting for someone to ask the right question. The question never came and the guilt had traveled back down into my stomach, lying coiled in my gut.

My voice was harsh. "I'm sick of talking about it. I have to tell the same thing over and over again to everybody. It hurts so bad every time I see it in my mind. I just want my head to go black so I don't have to see her falling anymore."

"Shhh, it's okay sweetie, shhh." Mom leaned over and held me tight. You don't have to talk if you don't want to. Here, let me lay by you." She climbed over me and lay down beside me on the bed in Verna's spot.

"Do you want some covers?" I asked with a hiccupping breath.

She said "No, I'm actually kind of hot. I'll just hold your hand until you go to sleep."

I heard Dad go into the bathroom, and blow his nose—he was getting ready for bed.

I asked "Mom, where is Willa now?"

Mom said "You mean her body?"

"Yeah, where did they take her?"

Mom took my hand again. "She's at Burton's, at their Mortuary. They're taking care of her there."

"Is anyone with her?" I couldn't bear to think of her lying there alone.

She squeezed my hand "Yes, they have someone with her all

the time. She isn't alone."

I didn't want to think about any of the other details of that place, with its dusty silk flower arrangements and weird smell of old flowers. I tried to think about Christmas, I tried to think about how it felt loping really fast on Lightning. I tried to think about anything but Willa lying in Burton's mortuary.

We lay listening to the crickets chirping and to the occasional sound of cars passing on the road. Mom began to hum the song she had sung to me and to every baby she had ever held. It was an old one that grandma had sung to her, one I had always loved. I think she was too tired to realize what she was humming or she would have chosen something else, but because I knew all the words, and they sang themselves right along in my head.

Oh don't you remember
A long time ago?
There were two little babes,
Their names I don't know.

They strayed far away
One bright summer day
And were lost in the woods
I've heard people say.

They wept and they sighed
And they bitterly cried.
Then the poor little things,
They lay down and died.

And when they were dead
The robins so red
Brought strawberry leaves
And over them spread.

Then all the night long

They sang a sweet song.

Poor babes in the woods,

Poor babes in the woods.

Mom drifted off to sleep before she even got to the end. But I finished the sweet sad song in my head, and all that long night I lay there without sleeping, heavy with grief and guilt, holding on to my Mother's hand. Watching Willa fall and fall and fall again.

CHAPTER THIRTEEN

A lost day

Mom slept beside me all night and I was surprised to find out that she snored. I couldn't sleep anyway and so it was a comforting sound. When morning finally came she woke up and turned over to see that I was awake. "Oh Effie, did you sleep at all?"

I lied, "A little."

Mom said "Well don't get up if you don't want to. I'll make you some cocoa and toast. You can have it in bed." She was trying so hard to be nice. She never allowed eating in bed. She left, shutting the bedroom door gently like I was a sleeping baby.

I was so tired. My head whirled with exhaustion and thoughts that didn't make any sense, but I couldn't turn my brain off. My arms and legs felt huge—ten times bigger than their normal size, too heavy to lift. And then in the whirlpool of thoughts a memory shimmered to the top, clear and sharp. My baptism day.

Willa and I were both baptized on our eighth birthday. The baptismal service was in the church, and we sat together in folding metal chairs wearing matching white dresses with sailor collars and wide white satin ribbons, tied in bows in the back. These were made especially for the occasion by my Mom. Willa and I were on the front row facing the baptismal font. Made of light blue tiles there were three steps leading down into it. A mural of Jesus getting baptized in a river of blue water by a guy wearing a fur outfit like Fred Flintstone was painted on the plastered wall.

Jesus had on a white dress and water streamed from his hair.

Jimmy Scott said a prayer and Aunt Holly gave a talk about baptism. Mom talked next about the Holy Ghost. I liked thinking about the Holy Ghost, who wasn't a scary ghost like in a haunted house, but not a friendly ghost like Casper either. He had a spirit, but not a body. I imagined that if my spirit wasn't trapped inside my body, it would look like my regular self only blurry, like looking in a steamed-up mirror. And it would be really light and feathery, flat enough to slip under a door or wispy, like smoke.

I imagined zooming around the world like the Holy Ghost, being one place and then another as fast as you could snap your fingers, without a body to slow me down. Mom said the Holy Ghost could make you feel good when you did something right or when you needed help, like a big warm quilt wrapped around your whole body. My Mom had a voice like a quilt, low and warm in my ears.

My father took my hand and led me down the blue tiled steps into the water. Gussie, Lizzie and all the little kids went forward to kneel or sit at the edge of the font. Gussie dipped her hand in the water and Aunt Holly said, "Augusta!" in her knock-it-off voice.

As I walked down the steps, my dress ballooned up around me like a lifesaver around my waist. I quickly slapped it down, worried my underwear would show. When we got to the middle of the font, my Dad looked down at me, patted me on the back and smiled. Raising his right arm to the square he held onto both my hands with his left.

Clearing his throat, he paused and I squeezed my eyes shut while he said the short prayer. His big hand supported my back, and he put his bare foot on top of my toes. Holding onto his hands with both of mine, I bent my knees and leaned back, supported by his arm , the water folding over me until I was submerged. I came up, blinking the water out of my eyes and let go of my nose. My father turned to look at Uncle Slab, who nodded, a witness that he had seen me go all the way under, with no clothes or hair floating up. My father gave me a hug and then took my hand and helped me up the tile steps to the fluffy white rug outside the font where my Mom had a towel waiting. Standing beside her was Willa, ready to go in next. My Dad was going to baptize her too. Uncle Slab didn't feel like he should do it because he never went to church and had a smoking habit.

Hugging the towel tightly around me, I watched as Willa went through the same process. Warmth spread through my chest, and tears stung in my eyes. My nose started leaking and I sniffed in an unladylike way.

Willa's baptism done, Dad helped her out of the font, where Aunt Holly was waiting to wrap her in a towel. Willa and I walked together down the carpeted hall to the bathroom to change out of our wet, white dresses into our Sunday dresses. We looked at each other and Willa grabbed my arm. "Effie, we're perfect, just think, right now we're absolutely perfect!"

I said "Yeah. Just think of all the sins we left back there, floating around in the water." We laughed, hunched together in our towels.

I heard muffled voices from the kitchen and huddled deeper under the covers. A sudden sharp pain stabbed my chest. I wanted to go back to that day—put on that beautiful white dress, hold tightly to my Daddy's big hand, and sink, water folding in on me. I wanted to rest on the bottom and then rise, sparkling, open my eyes and take a new breath, leaving the accident in the canyon swirling behind me in the water.

I felt myself sinking in the water again, and the font had no bottom. My heavy legs and arms pulled me down and I kept sinking further. I finally slept then, all through the day and through another night. When I woke Monday morning there was a mug of cold cocoa on the dresser.

CHAPTER FOURTEEN

How do I do this?

Verna went to school, but I stayed home. I was grateful because I had no clue how I was supposed to act now. Could I ever smile again without everyone thinking I was a creep? What about laughing? How long would it be before I would feel like laughing again? And could I ever show any emotion but sadness without people thinking *look at her, she didn't love her cousin one bit.* How long would it be until people quit staring at me and thinking, *There goes Effie. You know she was with Willa when she had that horrible accident. Maybe she is bad luck. Maybe something happened that she's not telling.* I felt Willa's death clinging to me like sweat.

Staying in my room most of the day, I tried to read "Little Women" but I couldn't focus. I tried not to think about Willa —and then I tried to remember everything I could about Willa. I tried to dig my earliest memories of the two of us out of my brain, but it seemed locked. Concentrating on anything was impossible. A thought would begin and then be interrupted by another thought sparking across my brain, making everything muddled and incomplete. Focusing on anything was impossible. Mom kept checking on me, trying to get me to eat or talk to her. I was relieved when she gave me a batch of clothes to fold. They were warm from the dryer and I piled them on top of me and let the warmth soak into me. I fell asleep and when I woke up it was already dark.

Verna slept on the couch again. I didn't say a word to her all day.

CHAPTER FIFTEEN

Curling Willa's hair

Uncle Slab called during breakfast to tell us that Willa was home. When I heard, I was glad for the excuse to quit rearranging my scrambled eggs. I put my tennis shoes on and ran over as fast as I could, not slowing as I climbed the hill. At first it felt good to run. My strides were long, my legs strong and fast. My feet hit the road in a regular, satisfying beat. But suddenly words sprang up in an involuntary rhythm with each step; *Will*-a-is-dead-*Will*-a-is-dead-*Will*-a-is-dead. My feet drove the words into the ground over and over. I tried to out run them by going faster, barely touching, but the words only speeded up and got worse.

*Willa*isdeadbe*cause*ofyou*Willa*isdeadbe*cause*ofyou. My heart beat faster along with my steps. I passed the twisty old halfway juniper tree. *Willa is never going to race me here again. From now on I will be going the whole way alone.* My feet took turns pounding out the word, a-*lone*, a-*lone*, a-*lone*, the rest of the way to Willa's house.

I was breathing hard when I came into the living room, and stopped short. I didn't expect to see Aunt Holly standing there. She was in front of a shiny white coffin resting on a silver stand with accordion legs. It stood in front of the big stone fireplace. Suddenly I felt cold, and started shivering as I walked toward her —my teeth even started chattering. When Aunt Holly heard me, she turned, reached out her arms and hugged me so tightly that I could hardly breathe.

"Oh Effie, oh Effie." She kept saying my name into my neck. I

didn't know what to say, so I just hugged her back to show her—
I don't know, that I was just—there.

It was a long while before she let me go and put her hands
on my shoulders as I turned and looked into the coffin. The first
thing I noticed was that Willa was wearing a white dress I had
never seen before, with a little round collar and lace and buttons down the front. Where had that dress come from? I knew
all of Willa's dresses, and this definitely wasn't one of them.
The next thing I saw was that her skin was really fake looking.
Where were her freckles? They had disappeared beneath a coat
of makeup. Her face was so familiar but also so strange. *That
was Willa lying in there!* I reached out and touched her cold cheek
with the ends of my fingers, then put my hand on top of her
hands, stacked criss-cross on top of each other. I felt her arm. It
was the familiar skinny shape beneath the white sleeve, but felt
heavy, like it was full of cold sand. There were no bruises, no cuts
—nothing to show why she was lying there so still.

Willa's red hair lay in beautiful waves over the white pillow,
but her bangs were all wrong, curled in a tight little roll that
went straight across her forehead. *Oh my gosh—she looked like a
first grader! Willa would never wear her bangs like that, not in a million years.*

Like she had read my thoughts, Aunt Holly turned to me.
"Effie honey, can you fix her hair? She would hate it that her
bangs aren't the way she likes them."

I swallowed. "Well, um, will it work? I mean... does dead
hair...or the hair of someone who is dead...I mean do you fix it
like regular hair?"

Aunt Holly gave me a reassuring pat. "Yes honey, it should
work exactly the same way. And you're the only one who knows
how to do it the way she likes it. Would you mind? I really don't
know if I could..." Aunt Holly didn't finish her sentence, just
looked at Willa lying there and started twisting her hands together. I could hear her knuckles making little popping sounds.

I said. "I'll get the curling iron."

Aunt Holly said "Thank you Effie, I think I'll just go lay down for a little while."

Heading back down the hall to her bedroom, Aunt Holly kept touching the wall with one hand like she was afraid of falling. I followed, walking slowly behind her. I stood in Willa's doorway and turned on the light. It looked just the way Willa had left it the morning she rushed to get ready for the canyon. That was only three days ago! It seemed like weeks. The old-fashioned white iron bed was messy with her quilt sliding off. Faded pink pajamas bottoms were a figure eight on the floor, where she had stepped out of them. Squatting down, I picked the crumpled pajamas, holding them to my face. They smelled like Willa. It wasn't exactly a great smell, but it wasn't bad either—just like her regular old self.

Dresser drawers were still hanging open with clothes spilling out. I opened the carved wooden box on the dresser—the one Willa's Grandma Jo had brought from Mexico. It was crammed with pictures Willa had drawn, old birthday cards, and notes folded into tight little rectangles and triangles. Most of the notes were from me, written during school, or passed during church.

I looked around her messy room. Willa's clothes and toys and all her stuff were still here where I could touch everything, see everything. I got down on my belly and crawled under her bed. In the dim light I could see a pencil, rolled up socks and wadded up dirty clothes. But no Willa. Willa was gone. Why did it still *feel* like she was here somewhere? How could things that didn't matter last longer than people? I let myself cry for a tiny bit and suddenly felt something soft touch my leg. It scared me so badly that I raised up , cracking my head on the underside of the bed. It was that mangy Uncle Kitty! Crawling back from under the bed I stood up, suddenly filled with rage. I kicked at him as hard as I could, lifting him through the air with my foot. He landed with a solid thump and darted out of the room. Stupid cat. He was a million years old and no one even liked him. Why was he alive and not Willa? It did not make a bit of sense. I wiped my face on Willa's pajamas. I knew she wouldn't mind.

I found the curling iron on the dresser under the mirror and beside it a small polished piece of petrified wood on a silver key chain. Willa had bought in on our third grade field trip to the Petrified Forest. She called it her pet rock and talked about using it to the hold the keys to the bright red Camaro she was going to drive when she grew up. I Slipped the keychain in my pocket. I took the curling iron into the living room. The cord was too short to reach from the outlet to the coffin, so I went to the laundry room for an extension cord. I gazed at Willa lying there in her coffin while the iron got hot. *Why didn't Aunt Holly stay to help me? Where was Uncle Slab?* The grownups had abandoned their place. I had never been in the same room with a dead person. But then again, this was Willa, not a regular dead person.

This was so weird. I didn't know how to curl a dead person's hair! *What if I accidentally touched Willa's skin? Would it turn all melty like candle wax?* My hands went from cold to sweaty and I wiped them on my jeans and took a big breath.

Standing on a little wooden footstool so I could reach better, I leaned over to comb out the tightly curled bangs. I would pretend that I was working on my old Chatty Cathy doll. I tried not to shiver when I touched Willa's cold forehead. Taking a small section of hair at a time, I rolled it into the curling iron, clamping for a second. It was so quiet, the only sound the clicking of the curling iron. I curled and combed four sections of bangs, carefully feathering them back with the brush. *It was working— this was going to work.* Willa's red hair shone, lit by the sun coming in the living room windows. As I finished, Lizzie and Gussie came clomping into the room and crowded in next to me on both sides, breathing loudly.

Lizzie touched my arm, "You are doing a very good job Effie."

"Yeah." Gussie nodded vigorously." Now she looks kind of normal."

"But she doesn't smell the same as she usually does, huh Gussie?" Lizzie leaned over the coffin and wrinkled her nose with a big inhale.

"Nope. She doesn't smell alive anymore." Gussie said, shaking her head sadly.

I said "Step back guys, you're crowding me." I put the curling iron on the stone hearth behind the coffin. "Gussie, hand me the hairspray."

Carefully covering Willa's eyes and nose with my hand, I sprayed Aqua Net over her bangs.

I stepped back; let out a breath I didn't know I was holding, and burst into simultaneous hiccups and tears. Gussie and Lizzie looked up at me with mournful eyes and both threw their arms around my legs. The attack was so fierce and unexpected that they threw me off balance. We all fell in a pile on the floor and I lay there sobbing and hiccupping, their arms clenched tightly around me, their rough little hands holding me, patting me.

CHAPTER SIXTEEN

Footprints

After I made a batch of red Koolaid and the Deckers came with the cinnamon rolls, Uncle Slab came in to visit with them in the living room. I watched him as he talked, his long fingers nervously smoothing down his graying mustache. He would quit for a second and then his hand would go right back up, like he couldn't help it.

Aunt Holly was still nowhere to be seen. Minnie was perched on the couch wiping her eyes frequently with a soggy hanky. Uncle Slab and Bill Decker were sitting in chairs opposite each other , both leaning forward with their hands on their knees, not saying much and avoiding eye contact. Men never seemed to know what to say like women do. After a while they get uncomfortable and fidgety and remember they have a fence to fix. I went into the kitchen and jumped when I passed the phone and it gave a shrill ring.

Uncle Slab called from the living room, "Effie, can you get that?"

I picked up the receiver. "Hello."

"Oh good, it's you." It was Mom. "How are you doing honey?"

I said "Okay I guess."

"Did you see Willa?" Mom's voice trembled a little.

"Yeah." I twirled the phone cord around my finger. "It doesn't really look like her, mom. Her skin looks weird. She just looks…" My voice trailed off.

Mom said "I know Effie, I know. It's because Willa isn't really there anymore. Her body is empty without her spirit."

I nodded without speaking.

She said "Sweetie, can you run on home right now and help me with dinner? Your Dad is washing up and we need to eat before he goes out to the Wildcat Pasture this afternoon. Jimmy Scott came home from school to help him fix a section of fence that's down. He wants you to come too.

I said "How come Dad's still doing regular old work and stuff?"

Mom said "Effie, you know the cattle have still got to be taken care of and Holly needs to rest right now anyway. Your Dad and I are both going to come back over there after supper tonight."

I looked at the food covered table. "People have been bringing bread and junk already Mom."

She continued "There's going to be a lot of family coming soon and besides, Holly can put what they don't need in the freezer for later. Now hurry on home Effie, and bring Gussie and Lizzie. They probably need a break."

"Okay." I hung up the phone and went back in the living room where the Deckers were heading out the front door.

I said "Uncle Slab, I'm going home for dinner and my Mom wants me to bring Gussie and Lizzie. Is that alright?"

Uncle Slab was patting his front pocket, looking for his smokes. Running his big hand over his face, he acted like he hadn't heard me.

"Uncle Slab?" I said again.

He jumped a little, like I'd caught him at something—like I was an alien that just landed in his living room.

I said "Do you want me to take the Missies to my house for dinner? Mom said to invite them."

He said "Uh, yeah. I don't think Holly's up to fixing dinner." I started to turn when Uncle Slab caught my arm above the elbow, giving it a squeeze. "You tell your Momma thank you won't you?" His voice was so kind, so unlike his usual distant tone. I had to get out of there fast. I was finding that nothing made me sadder than kindness.

I said "Okay, I'll tell her." Walking through the kitchen I went past the table laden with baked goods.

The air felt fresh and clean and I inhaled and closed me eyes for a second. I called "Gussie, Lizzie, where are you guys?"

I heard their voices before I saw them—squatting under the big cottonwood tree at the back of the lawn, staring at something in the dirt. The lawn didn't grow in the shade and there was a circle underneath the cottonwood bare of grass.

Gussie and Lizzie were facing each other; their heads almost touching. They didn't look up even when I stood over them. I said, "Hey guys, whatcha 'doing?"

Lizzie leapt to her feet and put her hand out to stop me from coming any further. Her voice was a shriek "Careful Effie, you're gonna 'step on it!"

I looked down at the dented metal garbage can lid lying in the mud in front of my feet.

"Step on what?" I said.

"Something *really* special" Gussie said, and her voice took on a reverent hush, "Something very important."

Reaching over, she carefully picked up the lid.

Underneath it were the tracks of Willa's size five Converse Red Ball Jets—two clear prints in the mud. The impressions were deep, side by side as if she had jumped from a tree limb to the ground.

Lizzie stuck out a proud chin. "We're gonna 'save them. We're gonna 'protect these tracks forever and ever so we can always remember how big Willa's feet were when she died."

"We're saving them for Mom for a present," Gussie broke in. "...to help her not be so sad."

"She'll like it, won't she Effie?" Gussie looked up at me, shading her eyes from the sun. "When she gets out of bed I think it will cheer her up a whole bunch."

My voice choked a bit. "I think it will. I like it a lot." Oh shoot, I did not want to start crying again.

"Do you want to come with me to my house for dinner?" I spoke brightly, changing the subject. "Your Dad said it's okay." They looked at each other and nodded, carefully placing the garbage can lid back down and then straightened up, wiping their hands on their jeans.

As we began walking beside the road down to my house Lizzie said suspiciously, "Hey, what did Aunt Lila make for dinner?"

"You're not having beans are you?" Gussie grabbed my hand. "'Cause you know we really, really hate beans."

"Because they make you fart." Lizzie pressed her lips to her hand and made a farting noise.

"No, because they taste sick, and anyway I'm telling." said Gussie righteously, "We don't say 'fart 'Lizzie, we say 'toot'."

Lizzie said "I heard Willa say fart about a million times. She says it about as much as she does it."

"Yeah, but now she's dead and gone to heaven and all her sins are washed away," Gussie threw her arms wide.

"No, it was when she was baptized that all her sins got washed away," interrupted Lizzie.

"And when we get baptized all our sins are gonna 'be washed away and so it really doesn't count if we do some sins before then, huh Effie?" asked Gussie breathlessly.

I said "Oh course it matters. You're supposed to try to be good."

"But..."

"Okay, okay. Yes, when you are baptized, all your sins will be washed away." I was not about to argue religion with these two. They would wear me down because the Missies 'religion did not include common sense. I would never win.

CHAPTER SEVENTEEN

Home on the range

World War III was avoided because dinner was green chili chicken enchiladas and not beans. Gussie and Lizzie loved my Mom's enchiladas which had the perfect amount of spice and plenty of melted cheese. I finally felt hungry and was able to eat a little. My stomach filled up fast though—it seemed to have shrunk. It was the most normal I'd felt since Saturday. I was perturbed to find that Verna was home, but didn't want to give her the satisfaction of asking why Mom had let her skip school.

After dinner was over Dad put on his cowboy hat and took out his toothpick. "Verna, we're going out to the Wildcat pasture to fix fence. Effie's going to come help, would you like to come too?" Verna didn't say anything, but her eyes slid around to look at me. I glared at her and screamed silently—*Don't you dare!*

Verna still didn't say anything and Dad continued. "We won't be very long and we won't work you too hard."

I stood up from the table. "Uh, Dad, if both Verna and I go, someone will have to ride in the back of the truck."

Dad said "I thought you liked riding in the back Effie."

"I just don't feel like it today, with Willa dead and all." This came out sounding really dumb, but I just couldn't help saying it. I would say anything to keep my distance from Verna.

Dad looked at me quizzically. Apparently he couldn't see the blood boiling through my veins pumping hate through my heart. I realized that Verna had become a repository for all the mess of guilt and grief that overwhelmed me.

Dad said "Load up girls. We're going."

When we turned off the highway we jounced and bumped down through one of the rutted roads that cut through our rangeland. Verna and I were squished in the middle of the pickup between Dad and Jimmy Scott. I knew Verna wouldn't end up riding in the back. The sky was uninterrupted blue, without a wisp of a cloud. It felt like a gigantic curved lid overhead, holding in my world. Out here on the range I could see for miles and miles, until the earth dropped off in a big curve.

Junipers sometimes crowded the road and scraped the sides of the truck as we passed. Brigham Bush grew here and there, it's long skinny green stems jointed like tiny bamboo stalks. Grandma Packer used to make very nasty tea out of Brigham Bush, believing it would cure anything. It was worth going to school sick to avoid it.

There was sagebrush, brittlebush and little clumps of wiry grama grass, very little feed that cows could actually eat. We had miles of rangeland to support our cattle. I had often heard my Dad say that with the sparse feed here, you didn't measure a ranch in acres, but in sections: each a square mile. Our cattle had plenty of room to roam and there were miles of fence to keep up.

I found myself growing sleepy, something that always happened when I was traveling with my Dad on a bumpy dirt road. I could feel my head bouncing like a rag doll, settling from time to time on his shoulder.

The pickup shuddered to a dusty stop near a section of fence that was sagging almost to the ground. Dad and Jimmy Scott got their leather work-gloves and the big old metal toolbox out of the truck bed. Verna got out of the truck and I lay down on the bench seat, warm with the sun coming in the windows. I still felt so tired.

A fly buzzed around my head and lit on my cheek, waking me up. My face was sweating on the vinyl seat of the truck. I sat up. Jimmy Scott and Dad were still at the fence and Verna was near them. Standing with with his legs braced, Jimmy Scott held the fence pole while Dad tightened the wire. Verna handed him some pliers and they flashed in the sunlight. What a little brat. She was trying everything to get them on her side. Getting out of the truck I walked over to where they were working. I couldn't quit yawning and stretched my arms out twirling around in a circle to wake up.

"Did you get a good nap, Effie?" Dad looked up and then twisted the wire and snipped it. "You really sacked out there for a while."

I said "I bet I could have slept even longer if it weren't for the stupid flies."

"There are always going to be flies buzzing around when there's animals, that's for sure" Dad said, straightening with a grunt. "I guess we're about done here Jimmy Scott."

Jimmy Scott ripped his gloves off, looking disgusted. "About time. I swear cows are the dumbest animals on earth if they're not smart enough to stay out of barbed wire."

He turned toward Verna and lunged, pretending he was going to put his stinky baseball cap on her head. She stepped back out of his reach and he slapped the cap back on his sweaty, mashed down hair.

I stared at him. Jimmy Scott teased me all the time and I hated it, but watching him tease Verna hurt. It felt like I had swallowed something sharp.

"Well, let's get back," said Dad. "We need to milk before we go over to Slab and Holly's. We ought to help Slab with his chores; he's got enough on his mind." He touched Verna's shoulder. "Thanks for your help Verna."

I climbed in the back of the pickup and froze all the way home so I wouldn't have to sit by her.

CHAPTER EIGHTEEN

Hey Willa

After we got back from fixing fence, Aunt Holly called, wanting Gussie and Lizzie to come home. Carrying a big pan of rolls covered it with a clean white dishcloth, Mom climbed in the car with dad and they drove off. I went to the barn to do chores with Jimmy Scott so I wouldn't have to be around Verna. When we came back in the house we took turns washing up at the kitchen sink. Verna was setting the table for the supper Mom had left us. We sat down and ate homemade rolls with butter, crabapple jelly and big glasses of milk. We ate quickly without talking. After supper Jimmy Scott turned on the The Flip Wilson Show, but even when Flip put on his wig and became Geraldine it didn't make me laugh. When the show was over I took a bath and got ready for bed. Mom and Dad still hadn't come home from Uncle Slab and Aunt Holly's.

I turned off the lights and pulled the quilt to my chin, thinking about how Willa looked, lying there in her white coffin. I tried to imagine my body emptied out of the part that was really me. Lying on my back, I crossed my hands over my belly like Willa's had been. I wondered if she was flying around somewhere, looking down. Maybe she was looking at me right now. Just in case I said, "Hey Willa." I concentrated, trying to feel her presence. Closing my eyes I whispered, "C'mon Willa. You know that if I died, I would come back and visit you."

CHAPTER NINETEEN

No phone in our hogan

Suddenly the door opened and Verna switched the light on. Closing the door she got her nightgown out of the drawer and said "Who are you talking to?"

"No one." I flipped over on my stomach, turning my head away from her.

Verna said "Yooch'iíd" yin it´ a´."

Navajo was a scary sounding language—every word sounded like cussing. Verna often spoke it under her breath to annoy me. I didn't know what she just said, but was sure it wasn't nice.

Verna took her nightgown and went out of the room, leaving the light on. I heard the bathroom door close. Out of long habit I remembered my prayers, climbing out of bed and kneeling down against it, my head in my hands. With a deep breath, I tried to clear my mind. Would the Lord even listen to someone keeping a secret like I was? Instantly the moment in the canyon played again in my head—Willa tugging at the stick in my hand—me pulling back. If only I hadn't loosened my grip. Or had I held on too tightly? I was the reason she lost her balance and stumbled back. *Willa falling, falling, falling.*

I shook my head trying to jerk the horrible thoughts out of my brain. Repeating *Heavenly Father, Heavenly Father, Heavenly Father* over and over in my mind, I tried to crowd out the poisonous memories. It became a chant whispered out loud "Heavenly Father, Heavenly Father, Heavenly Father." Hot tears stung my cheeks and I said "Please give Willa back, please give Willa back" again and again. The pain radiated from my heart to every part of me. It was unbearable. My whispers were desperate *I need my friend. I don't know how to survive without her. I need her more than you need her. Just start Saturday over again, wind it back. Please wind it back.*

I knew I didn't deserve it. But I asked anyway.

I was still on my knees when the door opened and Verna's nightgowned figure brushed past me, climbing into bed. I stayed on my knees a moment more, drying my face with the flannel of my pajamas.

I climbed carefully into bed, trying not to disturb the covers. I could hear Verna breathing, in a rhythm now familiar.

I said "Don't you want to sleep on the couch again?"

Verna said "No. I fell off to the floor three times." We lay awake listening to a truck as it came down the hill, watching the sweep of headlights pass across the bedroom wall.

I turned over toward her. "I bet you wish you could go back home to Lukachukai."Maybe if I suggested it a few more times she would take the hint.

Verna didn't say anything for a long while and then said quietly, "There is worse than here."

This shocked me. Verna *never* said anything bad about her reservation home.

I said "Why?"

She didn't answer. Another car passed and a coyote howled in the distance. With a sigh Verna turned over on her back and said, in a tiny voice, "My grandmother died this summer."

I couldn't believe what I was hearing. "Did you say that your grandmother—that she—died?"

"Yes." Verna's voice was small.

"When did it happen?" I asked.

Verna said "In June, when the corn was as tall as a dog."

One of the rare things I knew about Verna was that she really loved her grandmother. In the sparse handful of words Verna had spoken, or that I had paid attention to, this fact had emerged. There was a picture of her on the dresser, taken in front of their hogan, an octagon made of logs and mud. A small figure sat at a loom weaving a rug, her dark face wrinkled, her white hair tied with white string in a bundle low on her neck. Verna had told Mom that the yarn for the rug came from their very own sheep and that her grandmother was even teaching her to weave. She had never said a thing to any of us about that grandmother being dead.

I said "What happened?"

Verna said "She was at the hospital in Albuquerque because she had the tuberculosis."

I said "What's that?"

Verna said "Something that makes you cough and not breathe good."

I said, "Oh—I've never heard of that."

Verna continued "My Mom and Dad took her to the hospital and they sleep in the truck overnight. The nurse at the hospital say that Grandmother is doing good and they should go home on the weekend. So they come home for four days because they have to take care of our sheeps. When they go back to the hospital on Tuesday, they go to her room, and someone else is in her bed. So they go to a desk and ask some nurses where my grandmother is. The nurses say that she died two days ago."

I could hardly believe what I was hearing. "Why didn't they call you and tell you when she died?"

Verna said matter of factly "Because there is no phone at our hogan."

This was the first conversation I had had with Verna since Willa and now I was finding out that her grandmother was dead. I had never known *anyone* who died before. Now I knew two people! I closed my eyes and felt my brain twirling around inside my head, faster and faster. I felt very small. I felt very scared.

"Why didn't you tell us about this, Verna?" I asked.

She said "Navajos don't talk about people who die."

Puzzled I asked "Why?"

Verna said "Because if you talk about them a lot, then their spirit will just want to stay around. That is bad."

I said "Have you been really sad, Verna?"

She said "Yes." her voice barely audible." I have been mostly crying all last summer."

I asked "Did you have a funeral?" suddenly stunned remembering the glee with which we had hosted the glorious funeral for Finnegan.

She said "There was some prayers when she was buried and the medicine man sang some songs." Verna put her arm over her eyes.

My world had changed so much on Saturday, and now it had shifted again. I couldn't keep up with it all. How could it be that people you needed could die and leave you just like that—people that you loved. It had happened to Verna. It had happened to me. A new feeling hit me. Anger. It whirled into the maelstrom already churning inside me, just another strand blending into my sorrow and guilt.

And then I had another thought. Verna had lost her grandmother, but at least she hadn't killed her.

Something inside me seemed to unwind and break free, like a spring suddenly poking out of a mattress. A huge sob burst out and I wailed into my pillow, raising my head to draw in big gulps of air. Crying took me over and I didn't resist. I settled into regular racking sobs, sopping my eyes and nose with the edge of my sheet. It lasted a very long time. Verna lay quietly beside me and after a long while, I cried myself asleep.

Yooch'iíd" yin it ´ a ´ (you have lied)

CHAPTER TWENTY

I just love Grandma Jo

When I felt myself waking the next morning I fought it. I was still so tired—feeling like I would never get enough sleep. I squeezed my eyes shut, though they kept trying to open. Giving up, I peeked at my clock. Only 5:15. Even Mom and Dad would still be sleeping. Thoughts fell inside my head one after another like dominos. *What day was it? What was Mom going to make for breakfast? What were Willa and I going to do today?*

With a jolt, real life slapped me awake. *Willa was dead!* The cold fact lurked in the shadows of my brain, jumping out like a knife wielding killer to slash me with pain. *How long would it take before I really knew that I had lost her—when I knew it through and through, even in my sleep?*

I looked over at Verna who was breathing softly. *Was she dreaming that she was back in her snug hogan, sheep bleating nearby, her grandmother stirring mutton stew? Had her reality caught up with her dreams?*

Today was the day Uncle Slab's family was coming from New Mexico. Willa's house would be packed to the rafters with grandparents, uncles, aunts and cousins from her Dad's side. Even though Uncle Slab's side of the family was not technically related to me, I knew them all. I knew them down to the nitty gritty. I would bet you fifty dollars I knew things that my Mom and Dad didn't know. And Willa knew, I mean, used to know, everything about my Dad's side of the family too, but those were more everyday-boring types of secrets. My Dad's family tree

could not compare to Uncle Slab's side in the weirdness depart-
ment.

After breakfast I started walking up the hill to Willa's house. I
was almost to the halfway tree when I realized that I hadn't told
Mom about Verna's Grandma. Running back home I found Mom
on the front porch sweeping away the tiny brown leaves from
our empty willow tree.

After I caught my breath I said, "Mom, I forgot to tell you
something very important that Verna told me last night."

Leaves swirled as she swept them with brisk strokes of the
broom. "Oh? What's that?"

I took a moment, still catching my breath. "She told me her
grandma died this summer."

Mom stopped sweeping. "Verna's grandmother is dead?

I nodded. "Yup, she died last summer."

"Well I'll be." Mom leaned on the broom, brows knitting
thoughtfully. "She never said one thing about this. Is it the
Grandma whose picture is on the dresser?"

I told her everything that Verna had told me the night before.

"That poor family," Mom put her fingers on her throat like she
did when she was worried. "Not to know thing about it for days.
Poor little Verna—her poor, poor mother."

"And Mom, another thing." I said, "Verna said Navajos don't
like to talk about the dead."

Mom thought that over. "Well, I'll go tell her I know at least.
My goodness she has to have a lot on her mind."

"Do I..." I hesitated. "I mean, do I have to go with you, or can
I...?"

"No, you go on to Willa's. See what you can do to help Holly
before the crowd gets there. I'll see if I can get Verna to talk to
me." She turned to go into the house.

Relieved, I started back towards Willa's house. My Mom could
comfort Verna much better than I could. I felt bad for Verna, but

losing Willa was so big that I didn't have room inside me for anything else. I began to run.

When I got close I could see a pink Cadillac with a New
Mexico license plate parked out front. It had a "Mary Kay Cos-
metics" sticker on the bumper. A little burst of happiness went
through me because I knew Grandma Jo was here. Grandma Jo
sold makeup at parties and made tons of money. That's how she
got the pink Cadillac that Willa and I called "The Mighty Makeup
Machine."

I couldn't wait to see what color her hair was. Grandma Jo
could put more color on less hair than anyone on earth. She went
to the beauty parlor once a week and had it styled into a tall swirl
of cotton candy on top of her head. It sparkled with hairspray
and was so thin you could see right through it in the right light.
At night she wound toilet paper around and around the tower,
holding it with bobby pins. Her hair never got messed up, even in
the Arizona wind, as strong as a black widow spider web.

I walked in the front door and there was Grandma Jo, coming
out of the kitchen. She threw her arms wide and said "Effie!"
grabbing me in a big flowery bear hug. Grandma Jo was all about
flowers with bright clothes and sweet perfume. Right away she
started crying on the top of my head. I joined in, tears streaming
right along with hers.

I clung on to her nice squishy middle and we cried while she
rocked me from side to side until finally she drew in a big breath.
"Oh for Pete's sake, I'm making things worse, aren't I? You come
right in here and sit by me a while so we can cheer each other
up."

She took my hand and drew me into the living room. I didn't
know how we were going to cheer each other up with Willa lying
there in her coffin, but if anyone could do it, it was Grandma Jo.

Standing side by side with our arms around each other, we
looked down at Willa.

Grandma Jo said with a sigh, "Isn't she beautiful? She has always been such a beautiful, beautiful girl."

I nodded.

Grandma Jo let go of me, reaching into her sleeve for a hanky and wiping her nose. "And my stars, doesn't her hair look nice?"

"I curled her bangs for her," I said shyly, wondering if this was something I should be bragging about.

She said "You did? Why I should have known. Absolutely no one could have done them as beautifully as you, Effie. You did an absolutely wonderful job. You really did." She turned toward me, looking into my eyes. "I'll bet that was a very hard thing to do."

I shrugged because I felt tears closing up my throat and didn't think my voice would work. I felt for Willa's keychain in my pocket and rubbed the polished stone between my fingers.

Grandma Jo put her arm around my shoulder and we turned back toward the coffin to look at Willa some more.

"How have you been surviving?" Grandma Jo was still squeezing my shoulder. "I never heard exactly where you were when Willa actually fell. Honey, did you see the whole thing?"

I hesitated, "Uh, yeah…uh, we were there in the canyon and… we were…" I had never had to talk about the accident in front of Willa before. I felt as if she were listening, lying there with her eyes closed, waiting to hear how I would explain it all to Grandma Jo. I felt my heart beating hard against my ribs. my breath suddenly short. I couldn't stand it. I could not be in that room for one minute more.

I turned with a jerk, pulling out of Grandma Jo's arms, took one step and ran right into the back of a folding chair sitting near the casket. It folded hard into my stomach, knocking the air out of my lungs in a painful whoosh. I felt myself falling down an irresistible tunnel that went from gray to black.

CHAPTER
TWENTY-ONE

LaBarges at large

When I came to I was stretched out on the couch and Grandma Jo was putting a wet washrag on my forehead. She was sitting in the folding chair near me patting my hand. "Oh here she is. Effie, sweetie pie. How are you feeling? You landed flat as a pancake. My stars, I've never seen anyone keel over like that."

I nodded. I still felt light headed and my stomach hurt. My brain felt fuzzy so I closed my eyes again.

The front door burst open with the blare of many voices, all talking at once. Oh no! It was the LaBarge's. Willa's cousins from New Mexico were here. They were the absolute bottom rung of our long list of relatives. No one else came even close.

The LaBarges were rich and made sure everyone knew it. They had been to Disneyland seven years straight and the whole family had once gone to Hawaii for an entire week, coming back with Don Ho's autograph. They ate out at Denny's on a whim and lived a life of sophistication I could not even fathom.

Willa's family took me along for a visit to the LaBarge's home in New Mexico and I had never recovered. A huge basement rec-room held two pinball machines and a pool table on luxurious blue green shag carpet. Long shelves and cupboards were stacked with games; monopoly, risk, scrabble and clue. Rachael Labarge had a Barbie car with pedals and a canopy bed—and she was only four years old! Each Labarge kid had their own bedroom and their furniture matched.

Every time they came to Arizona, Willa had to hear about all the straight-A report cards, no-cavities and Pee Wee football championships. The LaBarge's were perfect and perfectly annoying. Willa and I had dubbed them the "Le Large" family behind their backs, pronouncing it with our best French accents.

As defined by Sear's catalog, the boys were all "husky' and the girl's were "pretty plus". Aunt Alberta was Uncle Slab's sister but that would have been hard to guess. She was tall, but unlike Uncle Slab she was thick from her wide shoulders down to her big square feet. She always wore dresses. Willa liked to say this was so people wouldn't call her sir, but if you looked at her chest, there was no mistaking her for a man. Instead of two mounds there was one big shelf of bosom. Aunt Alberta reminded me of a battleship plowing through the Atlantic with her wide rear end propelling her in the back.

Her children had the same build only smaller—and minus the bosoms. The four boys had blonde crew cuts, red cheeks, and matching tree trunks for legs. The oldest boy, Larry had a forehead so tall I bet Willa once that I could write the entire Gettysburg address on it. The three little girls had fat blond pigtails and beautiful blue eyes, but their faces were too small for their heads, features clustered in the middle with wide expanses of forehead, cheek and chin . Larry was the same age as Willa and me, which meant that all the kids were between the ages of twelve and two. There was an avalanche of noise when they were around.

A longing washed over me, making my eyes sting. I wanted Willa to wake up and climb out of that stupid coffin so we could make fun of her cousins together. How was I going to survive in a world without her? The team I had been playing on my whole life was now shorthanded, and I was going to have to forfeit every game I would ever play from now on.

With the house already filled up with company, Grandma Jo told me I might as well go on back home. There wasn't going to be any more cleaning or getting ready. She said, "The only thing left now is crowd control." because more family would be coming all day. Not everyone was going to be staying at Aunt Holly's, but they would all check in first, to hug and cry and talk. Neighbors and friends had volunteered to put up different family members that needed a place to stay. I wondered as I walked back home who was coming to our house.

Mom and Verna were sitting on the couch folding clothes. I sat down in the rocker.

"How are things going over at Holly's?" Mom shook out a pair of jeans.

I said "Okay, I guess. Grandma Jo is there and Aunt Alberta's family just came."

"Is that the ones named 'Le Large'?" asked Verna innocently.

Mom gave me a sharp look. Then she said to Verna in her no nonsense voice, "Their name is *Labarge*. No matter what else you may have heard."

My face burned. Verna had never heard Willa and I call their family anything other than "Le Large." She hadn't met them face-to-face, so she didn't know it was pure name-calling meanness.

Verna gave a tiny shrug.

"They are a very nice family and you will enjoy getting to know them all," Mom turned and gave me a glare "...because they are going to be staying with *us* tonight."

Perfect, I thought... *just perfect.*

CHAPTER TWENTY-TWO

The surprise

Jimmy Scott went back to school in the morning, Verna and I stayed home. Dad came home for dinner at noon. After we finished eating he turned to Verna and me, "When you two are done doing these dishes for your mother, I have a surprise for you." He put on his cowboy hat and went outside, the laundry room door slamming shut behind him. Verna and I looked at each other. A surprise? Quickly, we started clearing the table. I usually poked around doing dishes, enjoying filling the sink and playing with the bubbles while I stared out the window. Dish duty also inspired me to long bathroom breaks. Mom told me that as soon as my hands hit the dishwater, it automatically triggered my bladder. This was true. I was a slow dish-doer. Verna was not.

I had to admit that Verna was a worker—at anything she did. She liked to get a job done and go on to other things. This gave her an advantage when she did a job alone, but not when we worked together. Today was different though, we were zooming through. It wasn't often that Dad brought home a surprise. In fact I couldn't remember him ever doing it when it wasn't a birthday or special occasion.

"I think it is puppies," Verna was drying plates.

"Naw, we still have Queenie." Queenie was our ancient german shepherd mix, a fierce guardian of our highway-side home. Queenie was famous for fetching rocks. Throw a stick and she couldn't be bothered, but toss a rock and she was off like a shot, proudly returning it dripping with slobber. I said "We'll never get another dog while Queenie's still alive." I washed a pan and put it in the rinse water. I said "It might be a new bike for me." This was a mean thing to say and I knew it. It was also totally insane. Our family didn't have money to throw around for no special occasion. But I wanted Verna to know that if anybody ever got a new bike around here, it would be me and not her.

Finally, with every dish dried and put away and all the counters wiped, we were finished. Running outside to the barn, we found Dad oiling his saddle.

I was excited. "Dad, we're all done. What did you bring us? What's the surprise?" I could not wait another minute. What in the heck could it be?

"Hold your horses, girls. I'm almost finished here. He worked methodically, rubbing in the saddle oil with an old towel. He started whistling.

"C'mon Dad, you're torturing us," I jumped down from a hay bale. "We did the dishes fast and everything."

He put the neatsfoot oil up on the shelf and said "Well, come over here then. I'll show you what I've got."

He went to the passenger door of the truck and opened it. Pushing the seat forward he pulled out an old duffle bag. Made of green canvas , it had faded black letters on it. It looked like something from the army.

"What's in that bag?" I was through waiting.

Dad said "Let's go to the backyard and I'll show you. Old Matthew Dean gave me this yesterday because he thought you kids might like it. He's had it since World War II."

We knelt around the duffle in the middle of the backyard. The lawn was brown and the grass felt wiry. Dad undid each snap and lifted out a bundle of bright yellow shiny material that was rolled up tightly with straps.

"What is it Dad?" I asked.

He said "Help me spread it out and you'll see."

Untying the straps, he unrolled the bundle and started unfolding. The fabric was beautiful and sleek. Verna and I each grabbed an edge and backed up as we stretched it between us.

Dad whistled. "Take a look at that, girls—it's a parachute. This is the real McCoy—and it's made out of silk. They don't make them like this anymore." There weren't any cords attached, only the beautiful cloth.

It billowed and lifted in the breeze, the color of a dandelion. "This is the coolest thing I've ever seen," I said. "Can I really have it?"

"It's for you *and* Verna," Dad gave me a look as he headed back to the barn. "I figured you two could think of plenty of things to do with it." Sheesh, even the tiniest bright spots were ruined by sharing with my stupid foster sister.

CHAPTER TWENTY-THREE

Another surprise

Dad drove off in the truck and I directed Verna as we stretched the silk out as far as we could. It made a huge yellow circle on the lawn. I sat down to take off my tennis shoes and saw Verna starting to walk across it. I yelled "Verna, you idiot, take your shoes off."

She jumped back on the grass, kneeling down to untie her shoes.

The silk felt cold under my feet as I walked across the middle of it. "It's feels so slippery." I said.

"Slippery as a booger." said Verna, looking on as she slipped off her shoe.

"You're supposed to say 'slippery as snot on a door knob,' Verna," I corrected in a snotty voice." Sheesh, everyone knows that."

All of a sudden Verna went completely nuts. She yelled a string of mean-sounding Navajo words and rushed at me with her head down, butting me in the stomach. I was knocked flat on the parachute covered grass, too surprised to do anything at first. She plonked down, sitting on my stomach and started pounding me with her fists. Holy Cow, what in the heck was going on?

Verna's punches hurt and I started fighting back, slugging

and arching my back to get rid of her. I lifted my right leg and hooked it around in front of her neck, pulling her off of me. I rolled over until I was on top of her. She was still whacking away with her fists, so I grabbed her skinny arms and held them. I weighed more than Verna and it came in handy. I leaned over her, pinning her wrists down with all my strength. Twisting from side to side, she writhed, trying to get out from under me. We were both breathing hard and I could feel my heart pounding in my ears.

"Are you going to knock it off Verna?" I gave a little bounce on top of her to show I meant it. Her breath came out with a little whoofing sound. She turned her head to the side with her eyes scrunched closed.

I bounced again. "Well, are you? Are you? What's wrong with you anyway?"

Verna finally quit struggling and lay still. She turned her head toward me, opening eyes that were squinty and hateful. After a beat she said, "What is wrong with *you*?"

A powerful feeling surged through me, hotter than anger, deeper than sorrow. It felt uncontrollable, searing and volatile. My head felt ready to explode into a million burning hot pieces. Squeezing her arms as hard as I could I started screaming at her—spit flying. "What's wrong with *me*. You...you stupid...you *moron*! My best friend is dead! You stupid Indian! Willa is *dead*!

Then, quiet calm Verna did something I had never heard her do before. She screamed back—her words ringing in my ears. "Well *I* didn't kill her!"

I let go of her arms and punched her right in the face. I closed my fist, hitting her as hard as I could.. She cried out in pain and her nose spurted blood. I jumped up off of her and ran to the barn, cradling my throbbing hand.

CHAPTER TWENTY-FOUR

The middle of the sun

I climbed up the new hay bales, sobbing and shaking. Reaching the highest bale in the corner, right under the tin roof, I lay there crying out loud; I sobbed like baby first graders cry, with my voice and with my whole body. I couldn't stay still; I curled in a ball and then sat up. I pounded the hay with my fists and pulled my hair. Snot ran down my face, mixing with my tears and dripping off my chin. I let it run. I grabbed my knees, wrapping my arms around them, put my head down and rocked forward and backward, forward and backward along with my sobs. It hurt so *much.* How could I hurt this badly and still be alive? How could I? How could Verna say that? How dare Verna say that? She wasn't there. She didn't know that I...

I didn't mean to do it.

I scrunched my eyes closed at the memory of the surprise on Willa's face as she staggered backward. Her widening blue eyes locked on mine, not scared, just bewildered at what was happening. The surprise, the recognition that something was about to change was the last thing we had shared. Why had I held onto the pretend microphone? Why had I pulled against her? It was all so foolish and meaningless. Such a stupid way to die. And I could never admit any of this. The nonsense of it all was a whetstone that sharpened my guilt.

I cried until I was too tired to make noise and then I cried without noise for a while. Finally, when I couldn't cry anymore I lay on my side on the prickly hay bale, my body shaking once in a while with big shudders that came out of nowhere. *Would there ever be a day when I was through with crying?*

Something woke me and I didn't know where I was. The light in the barn had changed and there was a chicken by my head. I flipped my hand and said "Shoo." The hen spread her wings with a squawk and flew down to the barn floor.

I groaned. My body felt—I felt like an ancient grandma. But somehow I felt a little better too. I lay there thinking about what to do. As soon as I went in the house Mom was going to kill me for popping Verna in the nose, even though she had it coming —even though she started it. In fact, I was surprised she hadn't found me already. I was in terrible trouble. Maybe I could just live in the barn for a while—sneak in for food and blankets and sleep under a horse blanket. The skin on my face felt stiff with dried tears and snot and I was thirsty.

Okay, so I did feel a little guilty about how I had been treating Verna. I had been pushing her, punishing her, but—but what? I shook my head and sat up. I couldn't figure anything out any-more. Climbing down off the hay bales I went to the water trough, turned on the faucet and drank out of the stream. Cup-ping my hands I splashed cold water on my face then dried off with the front of my shirt.

As soon as I walked out of the barn door I saw the yellow tent. The parachute was draped over several wires of the clothesline— about three feet wide at the top. It was stretched out and pinned down with old bricks brought from the stack in back of the fence. The end closest to me was folded over and closed off, held with more bricks. That must be the back. I walked around to the front. More material draped down forming a front door flap.

I knelt on the grass in front of the tent, hesitated and then said weakly, "Uh...Verna, are you in there?" There was no answer.

I didn't move. Technically I didn't have the right to enter because I didn't make this fort. The age old unwritten rule of fort building proscribe that whoever built the fort was the boss. Of course, technically the parachute *was* half mine, but then again...

"You can come in." I jumped when I heard Verna's voice.

Pulling the flap back I ducked down and stuck my head in. I looked around in amazement. Late afternoon sun lit up the yellow silk and the air glowed with golden light. I held out my hands staring at my arms. Even my skin was gold.

Verna had spread out an old quilt and was sitting in the middle, cross legged. I looked at her cautiously. She didn't look like she was going to come after me and there wasn't any blood on her face.

"Uh, Verna—I'm sorry..." It came out in a rush "that I yelled at you and punched you and gave you a bloody nose."

"That is the number four bloody nose I had in my life." Verna sounded rather proud.

I said "Does it hurt a lot?"

She touched her nose "No, you don't hit as hard as my little brother."

"Oh." What was that supposed to mean? Verna had moved her hand to her mouth and her shoulders were shaking. Verna was laughing! She was laughing at her own joke!

"What did you say to Mom?" I asked timidly.

Verna was feeling her nose again, which looked a bit bigger than usual. "I didn't tell her anything."

I could not believe it. "You mean you didn't tell her?" *Oh, now I understood! Verna was going to blackmail me with this for the rest of my life.*

Verna scooted over on the quilt. "No. I am not a tattletale."

"So you're not going to..." my words faded off.

It was quiet and I started feeling embarrassed. I crawled all the way in and sat down near Verna, crossing my legs like her.

"Did you do this all by yourself?"

"Yeah, it was easy." she said simply.

"It's the coolest fort I've ever seen." I really meant it.

Verna nodded. We both sat in silence, looking around. I picked at the quilt.

Verna spoke. "In here is like the middle of the sun."

I said "Hey that's good, let's name it the 'Sun Fort'." *I wish Willa could see this.*

As if she had read my thoughts, Verna said, "Too bad Willa can't come over."

I stood up. "Yeah…it is." The top of my head just grazed the tent roof. "Man, this tent has a ton of room." Suddenly I was starving. "I am going to go get a cookie. Do you want me to bring you one?"

She said "Yeah, but not the raisin kind."

When I crawled back in the tent, I handed Verna two chocolate chip cookies. We sat on the quilt munching away.

Verna finished hers. "Who you going to sit with on the school bus now?"

I shrugged. This was another new and painful thought. I would be riding the bus every day to school and back without Willa! There was no end to this loss. I lay back on the quilt and put my arm over my eyes.

Queenie stuck her nose in the doorway of the tent. I said "Come here, girl. C'mon in here girl." She ambled in looking around suspiciously and then sank down on the quilt between us. I propped myself up on an elbow and rubbed her sweet old gray head.

Verna said "When my grandmother died I got to have some of her jewelrys."

"Wow, that is cool." *Were Verna and I actually having a real conversation?*

"And I got some of the money when we sold her sheep." Verna

said.

This was interesting. I said "How much?"

Verna said "One hundred dollars."

Holy Cow! I had never had that much money in my whole life. I said "What are you going to do with it?"

"I already spent some to buy my makeup." Verna slid her hand down the silky wall of the tent. "I bought some records too."

"Oh," This information was some kind of offer from Verna. This was an outstretched hand.

I said "Does it still feel weird knowing that your Grandma is dead—I mean, if you want to talk about it."

Verna said "At first I did not look at anything of my grand-mother's. Everything made me too sad. I did not go in our hogan except to sleep because her stuff is there. I mostly help with the sheep and stay outside all day."

I realized I could ask Verna the question—the one I really needed an answer to. "When does it quit hurting so much?"

Verna paused as she always did before speaking and then gave what for her, was a very long speech. "I think it is like when your finger gets slammed in the door. You are crazy because it is worse than your brain can think. You would like to be dead too, so you can't feel it anymore. Then, after a while it goes away a tiny bit. Some of the pain comes out of your eyes when you are crying. Then it goes away a little bit more and you don't cry so much but it still stays in your mind."

I interrupted "Is that how it is now, for you?"

She said "I come here from Lukachukai so I can feel better. I think if I come to your house it will feel like my grandmother is still at home on the reservation."

This made sense to me. I said "I can't believe your Mom and Dad *let* you come."

Verna continued "My Mom tells my Dad that will I learn a lot when I go to school here."

I said "So they wanted you to come?"

"Yes." Verna shifted, wrapping her hands around her knees. "But it is very hard for them, especially my Mom."

I said "And then, you come here and someone else dies." I turned over on my stomach and laid my head on my arms.

Verna's voice was very small. " I see death two times. When Willa dies it is like a door slams on my other hand."

Verna was crying! It was the first time I had ever seen her do it. She put her head down between her knees and her sharp shoulder blades shook, even though she wasn't making any noise. We both cried a while and I felt some of the pain coming out my eyes—just like Verna said.

CHAPTER TWENTY-FIVE

Don't feed the bears

The back door slammed and the sound of little feet slapped across the porch and thudded over the lawn. There was a rustle at the door flap and Gussie and Lizzie poked their heads in.

"Wow! This is supercalifragilisticexpealidocious!" said Lizzie as she and Gussie looked around with their mouths hanging open. Twenty-four solid hours of repetition had seared this word into her brain after watching Mary Poppins. She used it whenever possible.

"Can we come in Effie? Pretty please?" Lizzie clenched her chapped hands in the praying position.

"With sugar on top?" said Gussie.

"And sprinkles?" added Lizzie.

Queenie woke, saw the twins and got up, walking stiffly out of the tent. She was a smart old dog.

I said "Okay, but you have to leave when we tell you."

Crawling in, they squished between Verna and me on the quilt. Both giving off a smell I thought of as "Missie musk".

"Hey, have you guys been crying?" Gussie eyes went from Verna to me, and then she added quickly. "It's okay. Mom says we can cry as much as we want."

Lizzie nodded vigorously. "There's about a thousand people

over at our house right now, and they're all bawling."

Gussie leaned toward me, "But we came over here because we got tired of it."

I knew exactly how she felt.

"Is this your very own top secret fort?" Gussie lay back down with her hands behind her head. "Are any boys allowed?"

"Do Larry and Mike get to come in?"Lizzie asked. "How about Jeff and Buzz?"

These were the Le Large boys.

"No way," I said firmly.

Verna spoke up, "You have to stay out too, unless we are here and say it's all right."

"Okay," chimed Gussie and Lizzie together, and they both held their little fingers out.

"Pinkie swear,"

"Pinkie swear," we agreed, and I linked pinkies with Gussie and Lizzie curled her pinkie around Verna's.

I said "Gussie, who brought you over here?"

She said "Aunt Alberta. She and Uncle Virgil are hauling their suitcases in the house. Aunt Lila told them to sleep in you guys' room."

Our parachute tent would be a perfect tonight since the bedroom Verna and I shared was always the one given up for company. Jimmy Scott's bedroom would have taken far too much work to get clean for adults to stay in. The LaBarge boys would probably be bunking in there.

"Can we sleep in here with you tonight?" Lizzie begged. "I don't wet anymore and Gussie only does when she drinks too much pop."

Gussie said "That's a big fat lie. You're the one who peed last time."

Lizzie said "You're the liar. You're a liar, liar, pants on fire, swingin 'on a telephone wire."

I interrupted loudly, "Neither of you can sleep here tonight. The funeral is tomorrow and your Mom will want you home so you can get ready first thing in the morning. Plus, it will be way too cold for you little wimps."

Lizzie made a sad face. "But it sure would be nice to let some poor little girls who have just lost their sister stay with you."

I said "Where did you hear that?"

Gussie said "Lots of people say it. Everybody feels really sorry for us. So we tell them about how we are trying not to be sad because Willa isn't really dead, only her body is, and we will see her again and how it is really, really neat up in heaven."

"Yeah, heaven is supercalifragilisticexpealidocious!" Lizzie said.

We had a very full table at supper that night with all the Le Larges squeezed in on the long benches and a card table set up for overflow. Mom didn't have to cook because friends had brought food to our house as well as Aunt Holly's. There was one casserole that looked gross with lots of unidentified green bits, but there was also a big pan of baked spaghetti, covered with melted cheese. This was one of my favorites, but after a few bites I felt full.

After the blessing on the food, Aunt Alberta launched right into the Le Large family trip to Yellowstone. She gave an animal-by-animal list of every scrap of wildlife they had seen; elk, beaver, moose, buffalo—even a grizzly bear. Lester, the third La-Barge boy, had been most impressed by the smell. "Every geyser reeked," he said proudly.

I leaned over and whispered to Verna, "He should know." Verna glanced at Lester and then smiled slightly. Lester's nostrils were the size of quarters and I estimated that he could take in about 2.5 gallons of air per inhale.

Aunt Alberta said that Holly seemed to be "holding up" and that she didn't know how she did it. "Such a tragedy, such a tragedy." She began shoveling in her second helping, while giving a slow, sad shake of her head. Aunt Alberta looked at me every time she said anything about Willa and when she started turning towards me I would quickly look down at my plate.

She wanted me to be sad for her. It wasn't fair, I wasn't going to feel sorry for Aunt Alberta, just so she could turn around and comfort me. She could forget that.

CHAPTER TWENTY-SIX

Willa's favorite game

After supper the adults gathered at Uncle Slab and Aunt Holly's. They kept the littlest kids with them, but everyone that was school age on up came to our house. There were the four Le Large boys, Jimmy Scott, me, Verna and about fifteen other cousins. The easy camaraderie we usually felt was replaced by awkwardness as we gathered in the backyard. What in the heck did you do on a funeral eve? We had no experience with this.

Switching the flood light mounted high on the barn wall, we shot baskets at the hoop nailed beneath it, but nobody really wanted to divide into teams and play a game. Eventually wandering back to porch, we ate cookies from a Tupperware container, still wondering what to do next.

"Let's play kick the can," said Mike, a lanky cousin with a shock of white blonde hair.

"That wouldn't be reverent." Lizzie was always handing out new commandments.

"Aw Lizzie, we don't have to be reverent right now. We're not in church, and we're not at the funeral yet." Everyone looked at Jimmy Scott as he went on. "I bet Willa would want us to have fun. Remember how she loved kick the can?"

That was the honest truth. There was no one more dedicated to kick the can than Willa. She suggested it every time we had a crowd together. If there were kick the can in the Olympics, Willa would have been the team captain.

"Hang on" I said, running inside to the kitchen, I rummaged in the garbage until I found an empty pork n 'beans can. I turned off all the lights inside and outside the house. Someone ran and flipped off the barn lights. I planted the can right smack in the middle of the lawn. Only a fingernail of moon glowed faintly in the east, so it was plenty dark. Our yard was perfect for kick the can—with lots of good places to hide, but all of them a challenging dash to the middle of the lawn where the can gleamed faintly, waiting to be kicked.

Two willow trees sat at both sides of the back gate on the east, the fence made of wide boards easy to climb. An irrigation ditch ran just outside the north side of the yard, a great place to duck when it didn't have water in it, but the ditch was separated from the yard by a barbed wire fence. It was almost impossible to get through the wires fast without getting hung up or cut up. There was a hedge of evergreen bushes for cover along one side of the yard, and also a board bench built around the sandbox on the south. The woodpile and Dad's hay hauling truck were all great hiding places, within striking distance of the can.

Kick the can was fun unless you were "it". That job stunk to high heaven. That unlucky person was stuck with the job until they caught every single person hiding—it was you against the world. When you spotted someone coming, it was a pulse pounding race to beat them to the can and jump over it while yelling their name. Sometimes there were multiple attackers, so you had to be fast. But even if you caught every single person except one, and that person sneaked on by you and gave the can a boot, then everyone that had been caught beforehand got out of jail free and went and hid again. Most of the time whoever was it would finally get mad and quit. Then some little kid would be bullied into taking their place.

Gathering around the can, blinking, waiting for our eyes to adjust to the dark, Jimmy Scott shocked us all by saying, "I'll be it. Go hide. I'm counting to a hundred." The fact that Jimmy Scott, almost completely grown up at sixteen was even playing with all of us was amazing, offering to be it was unprecedented.

We took off in all directions as he closed his eyes and began counting loudly. There was no time for dithering. The best spots would be gone if you didn't make up your mind and run fast. I headed for my favorite, the willow tree furthest away from the can. When I was underneath the tree, I jumped, grabbing a branch with my arms and swung up. Piece of cake. I was an expert because Willa and I had been climbing trees forever. I shimmied out to the right spot on the branch, laying my body flat against it. From there I could drop straight down and hit the ground running. Another reason I liked the willow tree was because in it I had an eagle's eye view of the game. I could see who was where and watch everything that happened—picking the perfect time to make my move.

Good grief, Lester Le Large had climbed up on the roof of the house! What a dope. There was no way he was going to make it down the slick asphalt shingles without sliding off. Instantly I felt sick to my stomach with fear. I could not watch anyone fall ever again. Before Jimmy Scott could finish counting I jumped down, sacrificing my prime spot and yelled, "Time out Jimmy Scott." Pointing I said, "Lester's on the roof." Jimmy Scott turned and squinted at the large lump that was Lester Le Large.

"Get down from there Lester." Jimmy Scott sounded disgusted. "Don't be a jackass." Jackass was Jimmy Scott's favorite almost-bad word. It wasn't technically a cuss word at our house, but we saved it for when our parents weren't around.

Jimmy Scott walked over to the house where the roof sloped down to the eaves and called up to Lester." Scoot over here and come climb down on my shoulders." Facing the house he braced himself while Lester inched his fat bum until his legs were hanging off the roof and his feet touched Jimmy Scott's shoulders. Reaching up, he grabbed Lester's hands, balancing for a moment with the weight on his shoulders. Jimmy Scott was so strong!

Imagine, holding a Le Large like it was nothing. A feeling of love and pride for my brother washed over me. He steadied Lester until he jumped forward, hitting the grass with a grunt and rolling.

"How did you plan to get down from there?" Jimmy Scott threw his hands up as Lester picked himself up.

"I dunno." Lester said sullenly. "I was going to think of something."

Jimmy Scott said "Well go pick a smarter place to hide, and quit letting off those propane farts. The Martians can smell you." Muffled giggles came from the darkness until Jimmy Scott cupped his hands and yelled, "I'm counting one more time, so stay where you are or find a new spot."

I was disgusted with that dumb Lester. I couldn't go back to the willow now. All the good hiding places would be gone. And then I had a brilliant idea.

Running quietly all the way around the house I slipped in the front door. Making my way quickly, I passed through the living room and then the kitchen, feeling my way in the dark. When I reached the laundry room I crawled quietly to the back door. Slowly and carefully I turned the knob pulling the door open a tiny bit, squatting down and peering through the crack. I had a good view of the can and a straight shot, if Jimmy Scott didn't notice me first.

"...ninety-eight, ninety-nine, one hundred! Ready or not, here I come." Jimmy took his hands from his eyes. It was very quiet and then I heard a nervous laugh. This was a game you could not play with a full bladder.

The evergreens moved and two little cousins exploded out together. Jimmy Scott spun around at the sound and easily loped to the can before they were anywhere close. He waited until they were almost there and then jumped over the can once calling out, "Suzy" and then back over it again, "Skunk," before either of them could kick it out from under him.

"Wow, you two almost had me," I wondered what had gotten into Jimmy Scott. He was being so nice "You guys are pretty fast."

"I think it shouldn't count because you didn't say my real name." Skunk was a feisty little guy who got his name from the pure white streak that grew from a birthmark on the top of his head, clashing with the rest of his brown hair.

"Aw, c'mon Skunk" Jimmy Scott said. "I got you fair and square. You and Suzy are out. Now go sit under the tree."

They knew better than to argue with Jimmy Scott and both went over and sunk down with their backs to the willow trunk.

With a grunt and another burst of movement Larry Le Large was chugging forward like a freight train toward the can. Jimmy Scott, who was headed the other direction, spun around and with a few long strides had plenty of time to jump over the can, neatly dodging Larry who didn't have good brakes. Three down.

The cool October night brought a faint whiff of wood smoke and far away an owl hooted. Jimmy Scott walked cautiously toward the willow trees, standing between them, trying to make out who might be hiding there. Out of both ends of the parachute fort exploded Gussie and Lizzie, pounding over the grass. Those bratty girls! What were they doing in our fort?

Jimmy Scott whirled around and ran toward them, scooping them up before they could even get close. He had one girl under each arm and put them both down on the grass, tickling them while they screamed and kicked. He quit when Lizzie finally wheezed out, "Stop—or—I'm—gonna—pee—my—pants."

Jimmy Scott found or beat cousin after cousin to the can. There was soon a crowd sitting under the willow tree. I tried to keep track of who was left, but the only thing I knew for sure was that Verna hadn't been caught. Reaching into my jacket pocket, I rubbed the smooth surface of the petrified wood on Willa's keychain. *Where are you Willa? Are you watching us all down here? Do they play kick the can in heaven?* Then I spotted a slight movement.

Directly opposite me, on the back border of the yard was Verna, standing sideways right in back of the gatepost. Only someone as skinny as Verna could hide behind that pole. Jimmy Scott was headed my direction when I saw Verna make her move. She was sprinting fast and when Jimmy Scott heard her he whirled around and turned on the speed. He barely beat Verna to the can but didn't hear me coming from behind him. Sliding, I aimed between his legs and sent the can flying. A great cheer rose up from the crowd under the willow tree.

"You little..." Jimmy Scott sounded mad, but then his voice lightened up and he said, "Man that was tricky, you double-teamed me."

Verna and I were breathing hard, laughing, dizzy with victory and the admiration all around us. Verna's whole face was smiling; she wasn't even worrying about her crooked teeth. She was out-and-out grinning.

We played kick the can for about an hour more and then sat around on the grass—tired. Someone started telling stories about Willa.

"Remember when Willa made Ex Lax brownies and brought them to 4-H? Kyle Shumway ate about five and had the runs for a week. She never got caught, either."

"Remember when Willa made her own pinewood derby car and raced against the cub scouts? Her car kept winning and winning until they finally made her stop racing. She made all the dads so mad."

"Remember that time when we were branding and Uncle Jon bet Willa five dollars that she wouldn't eat a roasted calf nut, and she did?"

"Effie, remember that time you and Willa rode horses to school and tied them up on the monkey bars while you went to class? And remember how they left horse biscuits on the playground and you guys had to clean it up?"

We were pretty wound up by the time we got to this story all laughing so hard that Gussie had to make a run for the bathroom in the house, holding herself the whole way.

The stories went on and I realized that everyone's memories of Willa included me too. I was surrounded by cousins that noticed me, that took account of the things I did, both bad and good. The funny, sweet things they were remembering about Willa brought comfort to me, and a warm feeling settled around me for a sweet moment. But before I could savor it, guilt rose up, dousing my warm thoughts with the cold wash of shame.

CHAPTER TWENTY-SEVEN

Another goodbye

Only the LeBarge family ate breakfast in the morning. Dad and Jimmy Scott got up early and took care of the milking and did my chores, even though I didn't ask them to.

After Aunt Alberta and Uncle Virgil had cleared out of our room, Verna and I went in to change out of our pajamas. When Verna started putting on a dress, I said, "Did you decide to go to the funeral?"

"Yes" she said, pulling up her zipper.

We were slipping on our dress shoes when Mom called, "Girls, we need to get going or we'll be late."

It was only 8:30 when we got to the church and the funeral didn't start until 10:00. We went into the Relief Society room, a big rectangular space with dark blue carpet and white walls. Willa's open coffin was in front of a wide bay window hung with filmy white curtains. Uncle Slab, Aunt Holly, Gussie and Lizzie and Grandma Jo were all standing beside it.

A low murmur accompanied a group of people in their Sunday best, stepping through the double door entrance to the room. One by one they stopped at a small round table draped with a white tablecloth and a vase of flowers. A book lay open with lines for signatures. A small picture of Willa was propped on a easel beside the book. Oh, no it was her sixth grade picture!

She hated that one. She had been caught by the photographer with her eyes starting to close in a kind of sleepy look. Now here it was, a dorky picture representing her whole life. Sheesh, I wished Aunt Holly would have asked me about it.

Following Dad and Mom, we made our way to the second row of padded folding chairs. Our family didn't need to go through the line. I sat between Verna and Dad, watching. The air was sweet with flower scents, a big arrangement of lilies on the piano and several wreaths on metal stands surrounded the casket.

The people in line talked in quiet voices to Willa's family when they reached them. Uncle Slab would reach out first and shake hands. If it was a man he was talking to, he would reach out his other hand and grab a shoulder. Sometimes, he would give a brief hug. Uncle Slab wasn't crying but Aunt Holly was, her face splotchy. She hugged everybody, often wiping at her eyes with a white hanky. Grandma Jo was having a hard time too, and her Mary Kay makeup wasn't holding up, with some impressive black smudges around her eyes. Gussie and Lizzie were unusually serious, getting hugs, shaking hands and in between holding on to Aunt Holly and Grandma Jo's legs.

Some people made it through the greeting part without breaking down, but there weren't very many that looked down at Willa lying there without crying. There is something about a small-sized coffin that hits you hard. I had to take some deep breaths and Dad reached over and squeezed my hand.

At 9:45, Mr. Burton, the funeral director, announced that it was time for the family prayer. There were still people in line hoping to talk to Uncle Slab and Aunt Holly, but they all left and went down the hall to the chapel.

As Mr. Burton closed the double doors, the only people left in the room were family. He started talking, but his silky voice was so low nobody could understand it. Grandma Jo put her hand to her ear and said "You're going to have to speak up sonny, nobody can hear you."

Mr. Burton cleared his throat and tried again. "I'm so sorry, is that better?"

Grandma Jo nodded and got a fresh hanky out of the big black purse in her lap.

Mr. Burton continued. "Now we will join together in a family prayer and it will be offered by Willa's Aunt, Lila Packer."

I didn't know that Mom had been asked to do this. She tugged at her blouse and smoothed down her skirt as she walked to the front of the room.

I liked hearing my Mom pray. She talked like she did in regular life, not all fake and show off like some people did. I made me me feel like she was talking to someone real—like God was sitting in a comfortable chair, maybe leaning forward with his hands on his knees—listening.

She asked for comfort in our loss, she prayed that we would not forget this sweet little girl who had brought us so much joy during her short life. She prayed that we would all try to do what is right so we could be worthy to live with her again. She said thanks for a lot of things too, like the love surrounding us, for good friends and for faith that would see us through. A feeling of sweetness went through me, like swallowing a drop of honey.

The room hummed with deep amens when Mom's prayer was finished and I could hear lots of sniffling. She came back to her seat and Dad put his arm around her. Mr. Burton's hand glided through the air with an invitation for Uncle Slab, Aunt Holly, Gussie, Lizzie and Grandma Jo to come to the coffin to say good-bye to Willa one last time. As they stood, Aunt Holly turned around and motioned for me to come too.

I stood on trembly legs and went out our row and up to the coffin. We were all crowded together looking down at Willa. Even though she didn't really look like herself, I wanted to keep looking at her forever. Reaching out, I put my fingers on her fingers one more time. I spoke to her in my mind. *I'm so sorry. I love you Willa. I'll love you forever Willa.* We were all crying and Gussie and Lizzie were sobbing unabashedly. Uncle Slab bent over and rested his cheek next to Willa's and then kissed it. Aunt Holly did the same. We all stepped back.

I couldn't help hating Mr. Burton when he closed Willa's coffin. I imagined rushing at him, butting him hard in the stomach with my head and then punching and kicking him with all my might. Watching that lid come down was terrible.

CHAPTER TWENTY-EIGHT

Uncle Slab gives a sermon

The double doors were opened and everyone in the room filed silently into the long hallway. As I rounded the corner into the chapel I became aware that there were hundreds of people. The crowd stretched way back out of the chapel into the hall where there were row after row of folding chairs. All these people were here because of Willa! I had no idea she was so famous.

Someone was playing the organ and the crowd was standing as we walked by, turning up the center aisle towards the front of the chapel. I could feel eyes on me as I walked in with the rest of the family. Aunt Holly, Uncle Slab and the Missies, were first in line followed by Grandma Jo and the Le Large family. Dad, Mom, me, Verna and Jimmy Scott were next. A long line of more relatives trailed behind us. There were little signs that said "Reserved" perched on the end of several long pews at the front of the chapel. It was embarrassing to walk up the long aisle with everyone looking at us, and I tugged at the back of my dress, suddenly worried that it was tucked in my underwear. We sat down on the long wooden benches one after another. I was in the pew right behind where Gussie and Lizzie were sitting. They were wearing matching red dresses that had little green apples scattered all over and fat red bows tied on their ponytails. Poor Aunt Holly, she was going to have to fix their hair every day now. Willa had been doing it for her since last summer.

Willa's coffin had been brought in by a side door and was a few feet in front of us, at one side of the podium. It was draped with a big oval of yellow and white flowers—mostly daisies, and some dark green stuff that had a familiar, sharp clean smell. I realized it was juniper boughs, some with purple berries. I tried not to think of Willa lying underneath those flowers, in the dark.

There were flowers everywhere. Some were in vases and some were wreaths hanging on easels. I started to count all the arrangements but lost track when Bishop Turley started the meeting.

He welcomed and thanked everybody and told everyone they could sit down. He announced the opening song, which was by a choir of children. There were about 20 little kids in the choir seats, including some of our cousins. Miss Stump, who was going to be one of my Junior High teachers, was the conductor. She raised both her hands up high and as she scooped them down low and back up again, all the kids stood up together. They sang a song about being "a child of God, with parents kind and dear." Willa always liked that song.

I wondered if Willa was floating around here somewhere, listening and seeing everything. If I was dead, I would sure try to go to my funeral. I leaned into my Mom and she bent her head toward me.

I whispered "Do you think Willa can see all this?"

Mom squeezed my hand and whispered back, "I'm sure of it."

Dad walked up to the podium and said the opening prayer. His familiar voice was warm and kind, but I had a hard time concentrating on what he was saying because I kept thinking of Willa swooping around overhead. All of this felt like a dream.

Amens were said and I watched Uncle Slab approach the microphone to give Willa's life story. I could not believe it. I had never heard him talk in church and could only remember a couple of times that he had even *gone* to church. Uncle Slab liked to tell people that he would come back to church when they built a smoking balcony, because he couldn't stand to listen to an hour of preaching without a cigarette. Dad said often that Uncle Slab smoked like an old Chrysler.

He looked so handsome in his white shirt and dark brown western suit jacket. He was wearing his bola tie with the silver cow skull. As he stood at the podium, he put down the stack of yellow pages that his talk was written on and I could see the papers shaking.

Uncle Slab's voice sounded funny when he began to speak, like he had a bubble in his throat. He cleared it and started over. He told about when Willa was born and what a cute little red-headed baby she had been. He talked about how she refused to walk for a really long time, although she talked very early. He told a funny story about how one time she was sitting on the front porch swishing something around in her mouth. When her mom got suspicious and made her spit out, it turned out to be a stinkbug that crawled away, still alive. As he told this story, I could hear all those hundreds of people chuckling, a nice rumbly sound, different from the kind of laughing when someone tells a joke.

Once in a while, Uncle Slab stopped talking and took his handkerchief out of his breast pocket. After pausing to wipe his eyes or blow his nose he would go on.

As he talked about her, I thought about how much Willa loved her Dad. He had never acted disappointed about ending up with three girls and no son to help him on the ranch. She had loved his teasing and crummy old jokes. He had spent hours teaching her how to use a rope. Willa could throw a loop as well as Jimmy Scott.

He talked about how much Willa loved her little sisters, Augusta and Elizabeth—how excited she had been when they were born. How they looked up to her, how she watched out for them. I could see Gussie and Lizzie on the bench in front of me squirming with delight as their Dad talked about them.

Uncle Slab said Willa loved the outdoors and that everywhere she went from the time she was little she had been holding on to her cousin Effie. When he said this he looked down at me, paused and he blew his nose again. This was too much for me and the tears streamed down my face. Mom put her arm around me and held me tight.

He told some of the same stories that my cousins had told the night before. There was not one thing he talked about that I didn't already know. He was telling the story of my life along with Willa's.

I felt so full. I felt full to the brim with love and pain, both in exquisite measure.

Uncle Slab was getting to the end. Turning to the last page there was quite a long pause while he took out his handkerchief again and wiped his eyes.

He said "She was a mighty fine daughter. All her life she had people around her that loved her—and still do. She was a funny, brave little girl who lived and loved hard every single day of her life." His plain cowboy words brought Willa out of his heart, and it was if she was standing there before us.

Uncle Slab came down from the stand after his talk. He sat down by Aunt Holly and she leaned her head on his shoulder.

Aunt Heidi got up to play the violin. I had never really been too thrilled about orchestra music, but had always loved hearing Aunt Heidi play. She tucked her violin under her chin and drew the bow across the strings. Her playing was never scritchy scratchy—more like singing. I looked over at Verna and she smiled a little. I could tell she liked Aunt Heidi's music too. I asked Mom "What is this song?"

She whispered, "It's called 'Meditation'."

I leaned my head back on the bench and closed my eyes so I could listen better. Aunt Heidi's bow pulled the notes off the strings and set them soaring like arrows. There was no sound except the music—like everyone was holding their breath. Sound poured over us in torrents, a language none of us could speak, but that we all understood. It held the story of a whole life in it, beautiful and terrible.

The music seemed to be ending—a slow winding down part, and then a long pause. I thought it was over, and I opened my eyes, but the music started again. It was like the p.s. part of a letter, telling us about the unfinished part of Willa's life—about the years she would have lived if she'd had the chance. As the bow slowly pulled out the last note the silence was profound. I let out the breath I didn't know I was holding.

Gussie and Lizzie forgot they were in church and started clapping. Grandma Jo shushed them and a buzz of laughter broke the spell we had been under.

Bishop Turley gave the last talk and it was mainly about heaven. He told about Willa's first parents, who weren't Slab and Holly, but her Heavenly Father and Mother—how they sent her down to earth to get a body. He told about all the things that Willa had learned here, and how God wouldn't have let her leave us if she hadn't been ready to go. He said she must have already learned what she needed to know. This part was hard for me to understand. What was it Willa had found out that I still needed to learn? This was a mystery.

Bishop Turley went on, saying that Willa was happy now —back in her first home. She was with people she loved, her Grandpa Leon and others who were showing her around. He said that her big brother Jesus was there, and that he knew her by name. Bishop Turley's face was so kind as he told about all of this, and one time he looked right at me. I knew he believed it.

When he was done with his talk he announced that the closing song would be "God Be With You Til 'We Meet Again," and that Willa's grandma, Jo, would say the closing prayer.

I couldn't sing the closing song because my throat was too choked up, so I opened the hymnbook and read the words as they were sung. I really liked the last verse:

God be with you till we meet again,

Keep love's banner floating o'er you;

Smite death's threat'ning wave before you.

God be with you till we meet again.

I now knew firsthand what death's threatening wave felt like. I had felt it wash over me alright. It was a force I hadn't known existed. This past week I had been swept along in a flood of grief and guilt. Today, for the first time I had a glimpse of love's banner floating over me.

CHAPTER TWENTY-NINE

Bless this spot

We all got in our cars after the funeral was over and drove east of town to the graveyard. The town council had recently given it an official name, the" Pioneer Memorial Cemetery" in a big dedication ceremony. They thought it sounded better than "the graveyard" but it was slow catching on. Everyone I knew still called it the graveyard.

By the time we got to the place where Willa would be buried, her coffin was already there. It was suspended on wide straps over a perfect rectangle dug deep into the red dirt. Gussie and Lizzie kept going forward to look over the edge into the hole, and Aunt Holly had to keep pulling them back. The funeral guys were putting flowers out, in a big circle around the grave.

Cars pulled up to the fence at the edge of the cemetery and I watched people walk over the grass, the old people going very slowly. People called to each other, slapping backs and shaking hands. Everyone seemed glad to be outside, out of the church. When everyone was all gathered around, Bishop Turley announced that my Dad would sing and then Uncle Slab would say a prayer to dedicate the grave.

Dad brought out his guitar and he pulled a chair over, propping one leg up on it. His voice was deep and rumbly.

Oh give me a home
Where the buffalo roam

Where the deer and the antelope play

Where seldom is heard

A discouraging word

And the skies are not cloudy all day.

It was a perfect song for right now. I looked up at the blue sky and my heart felt like it was bursting. It seemed to take up all the space in my chest, leaving no room for breathing. I stepped over to Aunt Holly's side and held her hand. She was swaying slightly from side to side like she was holding a baby. A gust of wind blew leaves across the dead grass, and some of them swirled down into hole under Willa's coffin

When Dad finished the song, Uncle Slab stepped up, clasping his hands in front of him. Heads bowed and in the long pause before he began a crow cawed irreverently. In a voice clear and strong Uncle Slab asked God to bless this spot of ground, to keep it safe and protected, until his little girl's body was resurrected. It was a short prayer and as I said amen I suddenly felt very, tired, every bit of starch gone out of me. I wanted to lay down right there in the grass next to Willa and sleep sleep sleep.

The Burtons took the big flower arrangement off the top of the coffin and put it on the ground. Turning a small crank, the straps let out little by little lowering the casket until it was out of sight. With a slight thud it reached the bottom and they pulled up the straps.

Uncle Slab, Dad, Jimmy Scott and all the other uncles took off their suit coats, rolling up their sleeves. A dozen shovels appeared, and each man grabbed one, full of purpose, grateful for something to do. Someone took the green cover off a mound of dirt beside the hole and they gathered around it, waiting. Uncle Slab drove in his shovel, filled it, and threw it in, muscles moving beneath his white shirt. Dirt fell and clattered on the top of the coffin. Every man followed then, shoveling vigorously and throwing in a kind of rhythm. I was relieved when the coffin was covered with dirt, and the sound became muffled and soft.

Filling in the grave was a tradition in our community. I had asked my Dad about it once and he told me that it was a job no one wanted to leave to strangers—that it was the last thing to do for a loved one. Foreheads began to shine, and sweat stains appeared under the straining arms. Filling the grave didn't take long but most of the crowd had dispersed when they finished.

As Mom, Verna and I waited for Dad and Jimmy Scott to pick up their suit coats, I realized that something felt different. I had been stewing about how I would be able leave Willa lying there, underground. The thought wasn't quite as horrible to me anymore. The Willa I knew was gone—somewhere. And although I didn't know exactly where that somewhere was, it wasn't down there in the dirt. We got in the car and drove back to the church. A tired silence filled the car. Leaves whirled down familiar streets as the wind picked up, the bare branches of the trees bending.

A big meal had been prepared in the church hall. Long tables were flanked with chairs and the air was rich with the smell of ham. The hall buzzed with talk, a feeling of lightness in casual greetings after the somber funeral. The usual funeral meal spread out buffet style, baked ham and buttery potato casserole covered with cheese that everyone called "funeral potatoes". There were green beans flecked with bacon, fresh yeast rolls and a dozen varieties of cake. Relatives seemed to be enjoying visiting and catching up, pulling off ties and giving hugs. It felt more like a reunion now, and people acted glad to smile and joke again.

I ate a little but I had had enough of crowds. Turning to Verna who was sitting beside me picking at her cake I said "Verna, do you want to walk home with me? I bet Mom and Dad will stay a long time.

She chewed her chocolate cake and then swallowed. "Yes, but we'll get our Sunday shoes all dusty."

I said, "That's okay, Mom won't care today."

When we asked Mom if it was all right, she squeezed my

shoulder and said, "Sure, you two go on home."

As we headed out of town and down the lane that was a shortcut home, we walked side by side, but didn't talk, and I was glad for Verna's silent ways

CHAPTER THIRTY

A snowy Christmas Eve

The next week back at school was just as terrible as I thought it would be. Every part of it was painful, the bus ride without Willa, the cafeteria without Willa, her empty desk in English and Math and every slow minute of a never ending day. People were either way too nice, or avoided me. Marty Kizzar stared at me all through chorus like I was a freak. He kept it up until I rolled my music into binoculars and stared back at him. I was so tired when I got home all I did was pretend to work on my huge pile of homework, do my chores and go to bed.

It was the first time I could remember not having something to look forward to. Halloween didn't cheer me up, because I had never planned a costume without Willa. I felt like my brain and body didn't work right without her, like something had come unplugged.

Weeks went by, and time seemed to gradually move at a more normal speed. The truce I'd formed with Verna felt awkward after all the emotion of the funeral. We gradually settled into mostly ignoring each other. The weather got colder, making Willa seemed further and further away, left behind like the warm September days. The lump of guilt had settled into a permanent cold weight in my stomach.

Nights were the worst, my sleep constantly interrupted by distorted dreams where Willa fell again and again in a variety of ways, from skyscrapers, bridges, the top of a windmill or, most disturbing, Picture Rock. Always I was there, either ineffectual or complicit. Waking with my heart pounding I would lie awake for hours, going through options in my mind. My repetitive thoughts became well worn ruts as I imagined telling the Sheriff what had actually happened, being arrested, my family looking on with shame at their lying daughter being lead off to jail.

I was never without Willa's polished stone, carrying it tucked in my pocket where I could worry over it with my fingers. A little charge of warmth seemed to seep into my fingers when I touched it, comforting me.

On Christmas Eve the snow had been coming down on and off all day and our yard and pasture were completely covered. We got several snow storms each winter, but they seemed to miss the twenty fifth of December more often than not. Mom absolutely loved a white Christmas so she was in a wonderful mood. She was cooking in the kitchen and singing "It's Beginning to Look a Lot Like Christmas". I heard her tell Dad that nothing improved a dead lawn like fresh snow.

This year was Aunt Holly's turn to host the Christmas eve supper, but Mom had volunteered because Aunt Holly still wasn't up to it. I hadn't counted on losing my Aunt Holly when Willa died. She didn't seem like she wanted me around, and stayed in her bedroom with the door closed while the laundry piled up and the corners got dusty.

It was nice to have her here, even though I could tell her heart wasn't in it. We sat around the long table, covered with the Christmas tablecloth printed with red poinsettias. I concentrated on watching Uncle Slab eat. He filled his plate like an artist and his food always looked better than mine. He ate one thing at a time, going around the plate in a circle; turkey, mashed potatoes and gravy, corn (frozen from last summer's garden), fruit salad with marshmallows and a cloverleaf roll. After he emptied his plate he would refill it and start over. I admired a skinny man who could put that much away in one meal. When dinner was over, everyone except Dad and Uncle Slab were crowded in our tiny kitchen clearing the table, putting away food and washing the dishes. Maybe this would be the year Santa would bring us a dishwasher. Christmas Eve was really even better than Christmas because all of my wildest dreams were still alive.

Verna had been moping around since school let out three days earlier. I knew she was missing her family but couldn't understand why she wasn't excited about Christmas at our house. I knew she would get a lot more presents here than she would on the reservation. Her parents had even less money than we did, and I was sure our house was warmer than her hogan in Lukachukai. The weatherman on KDJI out of Holbrook said that the storm was so big it was covering most of Arizona. Verna would probably cheer up in the morning when she saw all her loot.

We finished in the kitchen and gathered in the living room for the program. Aunt Holly sat down at the piano and played while we stood around it and sang Christmas songs. We sang carols, alternating every other one with "Up On the Housetop", which Gussie and Lizzie insisted on. Their singing was more like shouting.

Every minute or two, Gussie and Lizzie ran to the window, wiping the steam off and looked for elves. I had grown up believing that after Thanksgiving, Santa's elves were on duty, watching me twenty-four hours a day, reporting back about all my naughty deeds. It had kept me in line until I was about 9 years old. At twelve, I was wise to this superstition, invented by my parents, but it was still working on Gussie and Lizzie. Jimmy Scott made it even more believable by sneaking out of the house once in a while and shaking a bell under the window. The jingling sound drove the Missies absolutely wild with excitement.

"Come look everyone!" Gussie pounded on the smeary glass. "It's snowing like crazy!"

Dad pulled the curtains back and we crowded at the window. A sudden gust peppered the glass with icy pellets and the air was white with snow in the porch light. I felt glad to be in my warm house with my stomach full of turkey and Santa on the way.

Our program always ended with Mom reading about the first Christmas out of Luke while the rest of us acted it out. We went back in the living room as soon as we had our costumes on. Jimmy Scott was Joseph, sporting Dad's bathrobe (which I had never seen Dad actually wear) with an old brown towel draped over his head tied with a folded red bandana. He was leading a donkey, played by Dad; who was flinching, hobbling slowly on all fours. I sat sidesaddle on his back, a soft blue baby blanket covering my head, wearing my new pink flannel nightgown with a little pillow underneath it at my waist. I loved being Mary.

Verna was off to the side wearing her matching pink nightgown with a white tablecloth over her shoulders. She was waiting for her cue as an angel, but with her sad face she didn't look ready to spread any joyful news.

Willa used to wear a burlap bag over her shoulder, tied at the waist with rope, a Lamb Chop puppet on her right hand to represent the lamb she was giving baby Jesus. Without her, we didn't have a shepherd. Gussie and Lizzie were both wearing the homemade crowns they had been working on. Their afternoon had been a whirlwind of cardboard, tape, staples and tinfoil. Lizzie carried a Barbie, who was wearing a matching tinfoil crown and a prom dress. Gussie, Lizzie and Barbie were the three wise men.

Uncle Slab and Aunt Holly sat on the orange couch, our only audience. Mom said, "Okay, is everyone ready?" Putting on her glasses she opened the Bible.

There was a knock at the door and everyone froze.

CHAPTER THIRTY-ONE

Will the cowboys fight the Indians?

"Who in the world could that be—out in this storm?" Mom took off her glasses. "Quick James, see who's there."

Dad was already at the door, and before it was all the way open, Verna was flying across the room, straight into her father's arms.

"Well, I'll be a monkey's uncle," Dad said. "Mr. Yazzie, Mrs. Yazzie, come on in and shake the snow off. And here are all your kids. Well, what a surprise, what a surprise."

Verna had gone from her Dad to her Mom, giving them both a hard, brief hug. The whole family was standing clumped together, inching into the room just far enough for Dad to close the door. I could see Verna's sister Carolyn in back of her parents but Verna's little brothers were hidden behind them.

"Won't you sit down Mr. and Mrs. Yazzie? Or come get warm by the fire why don't you?" Mom went right into good hostess mode. "How did you ever make it here in this storm? Did you drive in all the way from Lukachukai?"

"Yeah we did." Mr. Yazzie said, taking off his cowboy hat. "It's a pretty bad storm out there." He paused—just like Verna always did—a pause that didn't mean he was done talking, just taking his time with his words. "It took an extra hour or two." This was also a Verna-like statement. She never exaggerated—a trait I did not share.

There was another pause, and finally Dad cleared his throat and asked the question we were all thinking, "What brings you here?"

"Well..." Mr. Yazzie tapped his felt Stetson on his leg, shaking loose a dusting of snow. "'We just came to take Verna home for a little while."

Uh oh.

There was a rule, a big rule, an important rule—that all foster kids and their families promised to obey when they joined the satellite education program. Verna and her parents had agreed and signed a paper that said Verna would stay with her foster family during the entire school year, and not return home until summer vacation. Mom had explained to me that this was because when kids went to visit their families on the reservation, they usually didn't come back. Leaving in the middle of the school year put them further behind than ever.

Mom tried again. "Please—Nanette, won't you come in and sit down. And I bet you and the kids would like something to eat. How about a nice piece of pecan pie?"

Verna's younger brothers were finally making their appearance. Edging out behind their parents, both were staring at Jimmy Scott, who suddenly realized he had a towel on his head. He yanked it off.

Uncle Slab, still sitting on the couch, smoothed his mustache. "The kids don't dress like this every night, in case you're wondering. It's just on special occasions." He winked at me.

I had already pulled the blue baby blanket off my head, but Gussie and Lizzie left their crowns on.

Mom finally got Mr. and Mrs. Yazzie to sit down. Perching on the edge of the piano bench they looked like they were ready to jump up and leave any second. Verna took her older sister by the hand, pulling her over to the Christmas tree in the corner, pointing out the snowflakes she had cut out and hung on the branches. I got a good look at Carolyn. She was taller than either her Mom or her Dad, and very slender like them. I could tell she was Verna's sister; both had the same almond shaped eyes, turned up at the corners. Carolyn reached out an elegant hand to admire the snowflakes and set them moving in the air.

She had high cheekbones and full lips, her skin smooth. I touched the side of my face, conscious of my round cheeks, my sharp chin. As Carolyn knelt at the tree, her hair fell down her coat making a puddle on the floor. Carolyn was beautiful. She didn't seem to have one discordant feature. Verna took her hand and led her into the hall to show her our bedroom.

"Can we use your bathroom?" Mrs. Yazzie spoke softly and didn't look right at Mom.

"Of course, let me show you where it is, it's right through here," Mom said, leading the way.

Mrs. Yazzie followed her, with Verna's little brothers trailing behind. I realized I couldn't remember what their names were. I was sure Verna had told me.

Aunt Holly got up. "Girls, Jimmy Scott, come with me to the kitchen and help me dish out some pie."

Dang it, I wanted to hear whatever was going to happen next.

We went in the kitchen and I got down the little plates while Aunt Holly unwrapped foil from a couple of pies. Jimmy Scott took off Dad's bathrobe and sat down at the kitchen table. Gussie and Lizzie went over to the window and started huffing on it and writing their names. Ordinarily, Aunt Holly would have stopped them, but she didn't even notice.

I moved as close as I could to the living room so I could still hear what Dad was saying.

"Mr. Yazzie, you know We're not supposed to let Verna go home with you until the end of the school year."

No sound from Verna's Dad.

"And it's snowing like a son of a gun out there, it isn't safe to travel anyway. Why don't you just spend the night here with us? We'll all have Christmas together and you can visit with your daughter and then go back when the roads are better."

Still no sound from Mr. Yazzie.

"Now, I don't blame you for wanting to all be together at Christmas. I know I would feel the same, I really would, but I gave my word to the caseworker that I would abide by the rules. I'd just feel real bad if I broke my word."

I noticed that Aunt Holly was listening too. She stood there frozen, knife in hand, the partially cut pie forgotten.

Mom must have gone back in the living room because I heard her voice. "Please Mr. Yazzie, won't you and your family just stay with us tonight? We'll have a nice evening together and figure this all out in the morning."

Verna's dad cleared his throat. "I come a long ways because Nanette told me that we need our girl to come home for a little while. What Nanette says is the most important thing—more important than the paper. I am here to take Verna home for a lit-tle while."

There was silence and then I heard my Mom say, "James, can I talk to you a minute? Please excuse us, Mr. Yazzie."

They came into the kitchen and didn't seem to notice that Aunt Holly, Willa, Jimmy Scott and I all staring expectantly.

"James" Mom held on to both of my dad's arms, gazing up at him like we weren't even there. "...we just have to let them take Verna home. Did you see the look in Mrs. Yazzie's eyes when she hugged her? Rules are one thing, but what is right is something else. Don't you think so?"

Dad let out a big breath, shaking his head slowly. "Well, I sure wouldn't feel right about keeping a child from her parents. I know how I'd feel if it was Effie here." He looked over at me when he said that and it made me feel really good inside.

Uncle Slab came into the kitchen. "Well James, what is the plan? Are the cowboys going to fight the Indians?"

Aunt Holly whacked his arm. "Slab, this is serious."

"I guess nobody is going to fight tonight, Slab." Dad smiled. "Sorry to disappoint you. No, we're going to eat some pie together and then we'll make sure the Yazzies have good chains for their tires. They have a long night ahead of them."

CHAPTER THIRTY-TWO

A cold ride home

Verna and I helped Aunt Holly put pie on the plates and Jimmy plopped a scoop of vanilla ice cream on top of each one. We each carried two plates into the living room.

Verna's brothers were standing in front of the red brick fireplace, holding their hands toward the flames. They looked almost identical—about the same height with their hair buzzed off close to their heads. They still wore their red and black plaid wool coats.

Gussie announced, "One is Clayton and one is Thompson, and they aren't twins like me and Lizzie but I don't know which is which."

"Now don't point Gussie, you have better manners than that," Aunt Holly walked toward the boys and handed them each a plate. "I hope you like pecan pie."

Clayton and Thompson sank right down on the oval braided rug in front of the hearth and started eating. After he took one bite, I noticed that Thompson picked all the pecans off the top of his pie and put them on the side of his plate, and then continued eating the rest.

When everyone was served we all ate, looking down at our plates, the only sound the clink of forks and noisy swallows. This was not a talkative family.

I kept sneaking looks at Carolyn, trying not to be too obvious. She was so pretty! She sat on the edge of the couch, her back completely straight, and ate her pie with small graceful bites. She caught me looking at her and I quickly looked down, feeling my face getting red.

When I was finished I went into my bedroom where Verna was throwing clothes into her suitcase. It looked like she was taking everything she owned.

I said "Uh, how long are you going to be gone?"

"I don't know." She sounded excited and distracted.

I said "You're going to miss everything—Santa coming, and all your presents, and cinnamon rolls in the morning. We always have cinnamon rolls on Christmas morning."

"That's okay." Verna kept packing.

I said "Sheesh, I sure wouldn't ditch all my presents just to drive all night in a snow storm."

"Yes, you would." Verna's voice was crisp.

I realized that I had never spent more than two nights away from my home before. Verna was right, but I didn't want to tell her so. I felt like she was rejecting me, like she was rejecting our family and all the wonderful Christmas traditions we were going to share with her. My feelings were confusing. Why was I trying to get her to stay when I had been campaigning for months to get her to leave?

I left her to finish up her packing and went back in the living room. Gussie and Lizzie were huddled around Mrs. Yazzie, who was sitting by Carolyn on the couch. They were examining her wide silver bracelet, set with dozens of tiny oval turquoise stones in a beautiful pattern.

"Where did you buy that?" Lizzie ran her fingers over it.

Mrs. Yazzie didn't answer, but Carolyn said, "My uncle is a silversmith. He made it for my Mom."

Gussie gasped, "Someone actually made this? Someone you

know?"

"My brother." Mrs. Yazzie finally spoke.

"Wow!" Gussie said, impressed.

Lizzie was too. "If you *had* bought it, it probably would have cost about one million dollars!"

I saw Mrs. Yazzie and Carolyn look at each other and smile.

Verna came out with her pink suitcase. She already had her coat on. Everyone went around saying goodbye, making it quick because Mr. Yazzie had opened the door and sharp gusts of snow and cold were blowing in.

I hugged Verna with one arm and said half-heartedly, "Hope you have a good Christmas. Have fun in Lukachukai."

"Okay, thanks." I could tell Verna just wanted to get gone.

The Yazzies walked out to the pickup, Carolyn carrying a paper grocery sack with a loaf of homemade bread, a jar of currant jelly, and a tinfoil package of fudge. Mrs. Yazzie had a brand new blanket in her arms. It looked like one of the quilts my Mom made out of flannel squares that were pieced together and tied with yarn knots.

"Where did that quilt come from Mom?" I asked, as we watched them load into the truck.

"Shhh, I made it for Holly, but I can make her another one. They're going to need it tonight."

They did need it. The boys were climbing in the back of the truck, getting under a tarp.

"Are they really going to ride back there?" I was horrified.

"Yes, honey." My Mom had tears in her eyes. "They'll trade off once in a while with the girls so they can warm up."

"Man, they must have wanted Verna home *bad*." I said.

Mom didn't answer, she just kept wiping her eyes with her fingers.

When the truck pulled away, Dad came back in the house and

Uncle Slab stood out on the porch to smoke a cigarette.

"At least he has good tires and chains." Dad said, taking his coat off and stamping his feet on the mat. "And he said his truck runs good. I think he'll get home all right. He knows how to drive in the snow."

"Oh James," Mom said, and went and put her arms around my Dad. He dropped his coat to the floor and held her while she cried, patting her back.

"They'll be all right, Lila." He kept repeating, "They'll make it all right."

Mom pulled away and dried her eyes again. "But I don't think we'll ever see Verna again. I don't think she'll come back. Do you?"

"Well now, I don't know," said Dad. "I guess we'll just have to wait and see. I'm not going to say anything about this to old what's-his-name."

"You mean Mr. Squire, the caseworker?" Mom asked.

"Yeah—Squire. If Verna comes back—fine. What he doesn't know won't hurt him. If she doesn't get here by the time school starts again, we'll deal with it then."

Dad turned around and rubbed his hands together." C'mon gang, lets 'get our gear on and do our Christmas story."

Slapping his thighs he got down on all fours. "Here you go Mary, put on your head scarf and climb back on your old donkey." He lifted his chin and let out a long bray. Dad made the best animal sounds.

Everyone got back into costume and Mom got out the Bible. As she read about Mary and Joseph looking for a place to sleep, I thought about Clayton and Thompson, huddling under a tarp in the back of the pickup, heading down the highway towards home. When we got to the part where angels appear to sing "Glory to God on the Highest", I missed Verna—just a little bit.

CHAPTER THIRTY-THREE

Rules

We didn't hear a word from the Yazzies during the Christmas break. They just showed up out of the blue on the night before school started in January. Verna didn't say much about her trip home, but she seemed happier when she came back, so I guess it was a good thing that she went home, even if it did break a rule. After I thought about it for a while I decided that there were rules and then there were Rules. For example, I didn't think that God made the rule that kids couldn't go home and see their parents. A man wearing a tie and sitting at a desk thought up a rule like that.

God made Rules. They were more like, love your neighbor, be honest, things like that. The problem was sorting out the rules from the Rules. I'm glad I had parents to help me with that because it was confusing.

CHAPTER THIRTY-FOUR

Getting by

Every holiday that came was like a sock in the stomach, a marker of the first year without Willa. In February, Randy Brewer gave me a smoochy mushy valentine and Willa wasn't there to show it to. For some unaccountable reason, Randy had been in love with me since first grade when I beat him up on the playground after he lifted up my dress. Without Willa his eternally unreturned affection wasn't funny anymore. I felt defenseless. It wasn't the kind of thing I could share with Verna. We weren't fighting, but spent our days floating somewhere between indifference and tolerance

In the spring mom surprised Verna and me with Easter dresses. She had worked on them in secret, and looked so excited and happy when she laid them on the bed. They were made from the same pattern, but different kinds of material. Mine was a pale purple with puffed sleeves and little pearl buttons in a long row down the front. It had a high collar with a little fringe of lace and a white satin ribbon to tie around the waist. Verna's was yellow with white flowers. Mom said "Go on girls, go try them on so I can mark the hems." I took mine in the bathroom and locked the door, wadded up the dress and threw it on the floor. I felt anger boil up in me so fast that when I looked in the mirror, I expected to see my head explode. My face was red and I looked ugly. How could my Mom have betrayed me like this, making a dress for Verna just like she had made one for Willa every year? I splashed my face with cold water and sat on the toilet until Mom knocked on the door.

"Effie, what's going on? Doesn't the dress fit?"

"Uh, just a minute Mom, I..." I unlocked the door and when I saw her concerned face the anger turned into a sob that escaped, I could not hold it back. "Oh, sweetie." She put her arms around me and held me tightly while I cried, my arms in front of my chest, hands covering my face. "I'm sorry Mom, it's just that Willa can't...that she won't ever..."

"Shhh, I know, I know. I should have talked to you about the dresses." Mom's chin was on my head as she rubbed my back."It's just that you and Verna seem to be getting along so well now, and I thought that this would be a nice thing for you to share together, like you and Willa used to."

I pulled my head back. "It will never be like it used to be Mom."

"I know, I know." Her voice caught and she cried onto the top of my head until my hair was all wet.

CHAPTER THIRTY-FIVE

Cowboys make good campers

The last weekend in May we went camping. We usually didn't go until June, but school was letting out and my parents wanted take Verna before she left for the summer. She had never been camping, but then again, life on the reservation sounded like one big camping trip to me.

Camping trips were some of the rare times Dad did not work. There was so much to do on the ranch, and every day but Sunday was a work day. I was glad to be getting out of garden torture. If we hadn't gone camping I would have been spreading out cow manure for dad to disk it into the dirt. Planting would be next, which was okay but then the never ending hoeing and watering would start. It wasn't fair that Verna was going to abandon me to that big itchy patch of never ending work.

Uncle Slab and Aunt Holly's family were as crazy about camping as we were. The mountains of northern Arizona were only an hour away. We had our own favorite spot—a top-secret place at the end of very long and bumpy road—a campsite beside a cold stream full of apache trout.

Jimmy Scott and I were hauling gear out to the porch. I had learned a thing or two over the years about getting ready to go camping. Rule number one was: stay clear of Dad. Dad was the packer-*deluxe*. He could make everything fit perfectly and nothing ever slid around, blew out or got broken—but it all came at a price. He was as grouchy as a bear with a foot in a trap while he did it. No one dared say boo while he was loading up. I stood back, ready to do exactly what he said, but not ask questions or make suggestions. Suggestions really ticked him off. It was a great relief when everything was loaded, tied down and we were on our way after only three cuss words.

We were driving our embarrassing International TravelAll. My sincere prayer was that we would have a less dorky car when I was old enough to drive. The TravelAll was a boxy van that looked like it should be hauling prisoners. Uncle Slab, Aunt Holly and the Missies followed, their pickup truck loaded with more camping gear.

Now that we were finally on our way, Dad's bad humor gradually evaporated, and he turned into his usual friendly self. I leaned up from the back seat. "Dad, can you sing us the pig song now?"

"What pig song?" Dad loved to be begged.

"C'mon dad, you know which one. Sing it, will ya?" I said.

Dad had learned the pig song from Grandpa Packer, who probably learned it from great grandpa Packer, and so on. Adam probably made it up for Eve in the Garden of Eden. Although, come to think of it, I wasn't really sure whether pigs were allowed in the Garden of Eden.

Dad's voice rumbled out.

There was an old sow that lived in a sty
And three little piggies had she
Who tried while too young to say oof oof oof
When they only could say wee wee

Come brother said one little piggy one day
Come all of my brothers said he
Let's try while we're young to say oof oof oof
Though we only can say wee wee

These three little piggies they laid down and died

They died just as dead as can be
From trying too young to say oof oof oof
When they only could say wee wee

The moral of this story I'm telling to you
The moral of this story you see
Don't try when you're young to say oof oof oof
When you only can say wee wee.

Dad had a low gravelly voice and when he sang "oof oof oof" he sounded like a big old hairy boar singing from way down in a pit. When he got to the "wee wee" part his voice went high and squeaky. Real piglets don't even say "wee wee", which made it even funnier. The pig song even made Jimmy Scott smile, although he looked out the window and tried not to show it. From the wisp of a smile on her face I could tell that even Verna loved it.

CHAPTER THIRTY-SIX

The Swimming hole

The narrow dirt road snaked up and down for miles. One side butted the mountain; the other was a dizzy drop full of pine trees. I had to stare straight out the front window so I wouldn't get sick. I was proud I didn't have to stop and barf even once. Finally, we pulled into our favorite campsite. Whisker Creek ran through the most beautiful country in Arizona. Nobody else was there! Dad said, "Hallelujah Lila" and gave Mom a kiss.

Verna and I scrambled out of the car as fast as we could. I walked over to a huge Ponderosa Pine, stuck my nose right into the bark and inhaled.

"This one's vanilla," I said to Verna."

She looked puzzled. "Vanilla?"

I motioned her over. "Yeah, come here and stick your nose right here, in the bark." Verna looked wary, but came over and stuck her nose against the bark. She gave a suspicious sniff.

I said "Ponderosa Pine trees smell like ice cream when you sniff the bark right up close. Some trees smell like chocolate, some like strawberry, and some vanilla."

"Wow" said Verna. "It really does." It made me feel good to teach Verna something about the outdoors, because everyone knows how Indians are one with nature.

The forest was full of other trees too, and Mom started pointing them out: Blue Spruce, Gambel Oak, Shaking Leaf Aspen, and Alligator Bark Juniper. The air was cool, sharp with the smell of pine, but my favorite thing was the sound of Whisker Creek. When you lived and ranched on the dry, high desert like we did, water running over rocks sounded as pretty as Dionne Warwick singing. I had never been to a big river, and imagined that it would sound more like Ed Ames, deep and low. Ed Ames was my personal crush, appearing weekly on Daniel Boone as Mingo. Whisker Creek definitely had the voice of a woman.

Everyone was anxious to unload and we set up camp fast. First we all helped pitch two green army tents for Mom and Dad and Uncle Slab and Aunt Holly. Jimmy Scott put up the pup tent he got when he was a Boy Scout and Verna and I wrestled with the four man tent. It was a shame we had to share it with the Missies. I tried to talk Aunt Holly into letting them sleep with her and Uncle Slab, but got absolutely nowhere.

After quick peanut butter and jelly sandwiches, Uncle Slab, Dad and Jimmy Scott headed downstream to fish and all the girls hiked upstream to our favorite swimming hole. It was the deepest place in the creek, and one of the reasons we camped nearby. It always looked a little different, depending on how high the creek was and what had happened over the winter months. There were big boulders to jump off, all of which we had named.

I pointed them out to Verna. Booger was the baby jump, a small boulder a few feet above the water that was covered with gray-green stuff Mom called lichen. Jumping from Booger took no courage and was for beginners. A few yards away, Ollie, curved back about six feet above the water. It took a smidgen of guts to jump off Ollie and I had even dared to dive a few times. The next highest launching place was Aunt Bea, which was across the creek on the other side of the swimming hole. Aunt Bea was the name of the jumping-off spot, but to get to it you climbed up a split in the rock that Jimmy had named, "Aunt Bea's crack". We only called it that when our parents couldn't hear us. I had jumped from Aunt Bea only one time and it about scared the pants off me, but Willa had done it a bunch of times. She had always been braver than me.

The highest jump of all was Dragon—short for Dragon's Head. It was on the same side of the creek as Aunt Bea, only higher. Only Jimmy Scott had jumped from Dragon, and every time he did Mom's lips got tight, and she would close her eyes and squeeze her fists until it was over. It made her mad that Dad let him do it. Dad said it was probably thirty feet high—Jimmy Scott argued that it was more like forty. All I knew was that I'd never have the guts to jump from way up there. I had climbed up to it just once, and looking at the water far below had made me feel like fainting. I never climbed up there again because it had been very scary getting back down.

Verna and I peeled off our clothes to the swimming suits underneath. I already knew the water was icy cold and I felt shivery all over thinking about the first jump. I climbed up on Ollie, paused at the edge and yelled, "Ooooo Baby!" as I sprang way out into the air and did a cannonball. When I hit, holding on to one knee, a spray of water boomed way up in the air. I came up choking and laughing—splashing around to warm myself. Verna jumped in right after me, her body straight, hands at her sides in a pencil jump. This was quite brave of her because this took her way down under where the water was the very coldest. She kicked to the top and shot up out of the water with a scream.

"Verna, stop that!" Mom scolded. "Someone will think you're hurt."

"It does hurt," I shouted back at Mom, trying to splash some cold water on her so she would know how it felt. "We're about to have heart attacks from freezingness."

"You are a weenie," Verna said as she dog paddled to the side.

I lunged toward her in the water, trying to dunk her before she could get out but wasn't fast enough. I climbed out right behind her and we lay back on a flat, dry boulder, warming up for another jump. I said "I thought you didn't like to swim. Remember you said that when Jill had her pool party?"

Verna squeezed water out of her hair and said "I don't like to swim in pools full of kid pee." I had to admit, she had a point.

Gussie and Lizzie were at the edge of the pool, poking their big toes in the water and then running back, with exaggerated shivers. I knew they were too wimpy to get all the way in.

Mom and Aunt Holly had stripped down to their swimsuits and were sitting on a warm rock watching the twins and talking. They never ran out of things to talk about and sometimes their conversations were quite interesting. Willa and I had learned a lot this by looking like we weren't paying attention when they were talking about juicy stuff. Today though, the talk was about some Doctor Spock who knew everything about raising kids.

"Holy Cow!" I whispered, as Verna turned her head toward me. "They are actually talking about potty training, and they don't even have babies! Why do moms like to talk about poop so much? I hope I never get that boring."

She nodded. "It is very sad."

After jumping from Ollie a few more times, Verna and I spread out the patchwork denim quilt. I lay back, covered with goose bumps, but soon I could feel the warm boulder beneath me sucking the cold out of my body.

"I wonder if your Dad and Jimmy Scott will catch any fish." Verna said as she shifted on the rock.

"Even if they don't they will still talk about it for hours." I said. "I don't get what is so exciting about fishing and I 'm definitely not going to eat the stinky things. I hate fish." I made a face.

Verna sniffed. "You have a cow prejudice. You need to try some mutton."

"Is that sheep meat?" I asked.

She said "Yeah. Mutton stew is really good, especially with fry bread."

I propped up on one elbow and turned toward Verna." Mom never cooks anything but beef because our freezer is packed full of it. We're still eating Jimmy Scott's steer that we had to butcher when it broke its leg trying to jump the fence. I bet it would have won grand champion at the Navajo County Fair if he hadn't done that. Man, that steer was wild!"

I turned over on my stomach so the sun could get to my back. "None of the meat in our freezer is from cows butchered on purpose. They all died accidentally."

After a few minutes I was getting dry and feeling too hot, "C'mon, let's get back in. I'm ready, are you?"

We both jumped off Booger and splashed around in the cold water. Paddling close Verna said, "I'm going to climb up and jump off those other rocks. You can come if you want." She swam to the other side of the pool and pulled herself out.

Climbing up there was the last thing I wanted to do. What was Verna thinking? I swam back to the rock with the quilt and climbed out, shivering. My heart started to race.

CHAPTER THIRTY-SEVEN

Dragon

I looked over at Mom and Aunt Holly. They were chatting away, watching the Missies. They weren't paying any attention to either me or Verna.

She was bracing herself in the cleft of the rock, climbing swiftly, like she had done it lots of times before. I breathed a sigh of relief when she got to the big jumping off spot we called Aunt Bea. But then she turned around and kept climbing.

She was out of sight during the last few yards to the top of Dragon. I felt like I was going to barf. I opened my mouth to tattle to Mom and Aunt Holly so they would make her stop but no words came out. I put my head down on my knees and squeezed my eyes shut. And then I heard her voice, "Hey guys!" I scrambled to my feet and had to shade my eyes to see her silhouetted above me. Verna moved a little on the edge, blocking out the sun for just a second, and then she yelled, "Geronimo!" springing way out in her red suit as Mom and Aunt Holly jumped to their feet, too late to stop her. I knew they were shouting but suddenly sound seemed to shut off as Verna came down. She looked beautiful, her skinny brown arms and legs curved against the blue sky, her wet hair flying up in black sticks.

I saw her hit the water holding her nose and then everything went kind of fuzzy and I smacked down hard on my bum. I could feel my heart in my chest, fast hammering against my ribs. I saw quick flashes of images in my head—now it was Willa falling but her hair was straight and black like Verna's. Suddenly it was Verna laughing at me as she jumped from Picture Rock. Then it was Willa laughing, holding hands with Verna as they jumped together. I couldn't catch my breath as I tried to stand, struggling to get air into my lungs, staggered.

The shock of the cold water hit me like a slap. Thrashing to the surface, I choked on the mouthful of water I had gulped when I fell in. I kicked and coughed, ignoring Verna who was grinning and dog paddling beside me.

"Girls! Both of you! Out of the water this instant!" Mom's voice sliced through the air like a javelin. Aunt Holly's angry voice joined in and both women were yelling and waving their arms. I couldn't hear them. Climbing out of the water, a roaring sound filled my ears and anger coursed so hot and painfully it felt like my head was full of lava. I turned and walked away.

By the time I got back to camp the pain of my bare feet finally got through to me. I ducked into the tent and collapsed on the green sleeping bag still crumpled where I had left it. I examined my sore feet and picked out stickers, brushing off dirt and gravelly bits. My tender feet throbbed with the effects of the half mile hike from the swimming hole. But the pain seemed welcome somehow. At least the pain was real. It brought me back from wherever it was that my mind had peeled off to when Verna jumped. My heart began to race again as I saw her plummet and sweat flushed my face and body. I tucked my head and wrapped my arms around my knees, rocking forward and back, forward and back.

I don't know when I fell asleep, I didn't wake until my Mom poked her head in the tent. "Effie honey, are you alright?" I rolled over and sat up and said "I don't feel very good". Mom ducked through the tent door and came over to kneel beside my sleeping bag. She put her cool hand on my forehead. "You probably got a little too much sun." I nodded. She said "Did Verna's jump upset you?" I didn't answer, but could feel my heart speed up again.

Mom smoothed my hair back from my forehead. "She shouldn't have done that Effie. Believe me; she got a good talking to. I swear, I don't know what gets into you girls sometimes. You just go ahead and stay here until you feel better. We're going to work on supper."

CHAPTER THIRTY-EIGHT

Verna speaks

I didn't come out to eat, even though the smell of hot biscuits wafting from the dutch oven was about my favorite thing in the world. I felt drained and heavy at the same time, too weak to lift myself up and out of the tent.

It was about ten thirty by the time everyone finally settled down for the night. The Missies were asleep before they had a chance to turn over. I snuggled down in my sleeping bag, watching the tent fabric ripple, the night breeze cool.

"Are you asleep?" Verna knew I wasn't.

I let a long pause stretch before I said "No." I still felt so angry with Verna.

"I'm sorry that I jumped off Dragon." Verna turned on her side towards me. I didn't answer and the grudging silence stretched out between us. Finally I asked, "Why did you do it?"

A coyote barked in the distance and then howled, a thin sound, mournful and eerie. Verna said, "I don't know. I didn't plan on it; I just kept climbing until I got to the top."

"You are so stupid Verna, you know that?"

Verna didn't answer. The coyote sounded again, joined by other howls that twisted in a lonely chord. I shivered.

Verna said "Are you scared of coyotes?"

Now it was my turn to play the no talk game. I let the silence stretch to give Verna a taste of her own medicine.

She said "I like coyotes. My grandmother used to tell me the story of how coyote killed a giant."

I really wanted to hear this story, but didn't want to give up the advantage of my silence and Verna's willingness to talk. It was power I rarely held. "Huh" I said noncommittally.

"There was a coyote who was wandering all over the place" Verna said leaning up on one elbow. "He was searching for a giant that was killing everyone. After looking around for a long time, the coyote found out that he was already inside the giant's belly."

I couldn't help myself, I blurted out, "How did that happen?"

Verna continued "The coyote thought he had gone inside a cave, but it was really the giant's mouth. There were lots of other animals all trapped inside the giant's belly with the coyote. After a while he came up with a plan. He started eating the giant's heart, a little at a time until the giant was finally so weak the coyote was able to help all the animals to escape as the giant took his last breath." Verna lay back down and pulled her arms inside the sleeping bag.

I said, "Sorry, but I still hate coyotes." One of the twins murmured something in her sleep and let out a soft huffing sound.

Verna said, "I wish my grandmother had a funeral like Willa did."

This was weird, didn't everybody have a funeral? I said, "I've been to a few of them, but Willa's was the first for someone, you know—like us."

Suddenly, the guilt that had laid heavy for months uncoiled within me. It sprang up my throat with the caustic acid of vomit. It was so sudden, so powerful and so unexpected after tamping it down for so long. I began to sob, ducked my head down in the sleeping bag to muffle the sound. I cried into the soft flannel, holding it against my mouth to muffle my cries, soaking it with my tears. Verna said nothing. She lay quietly waiting.

"Verna," my voice sounded weird because my nose was completely plugged with snot "...remember when we had that fight —and I uh, gave you a bloody nose?"

Verna shifted in her sleeping bag. "Yeah."

I continued "Do you remember what you said, how you said that—that *you* didn't kill Willa?"

"Yeah, I remember." Verna reached up and stroked the side of the tent with her fingertips.

I turned over on my stomach and got up on both elbows, trying to see her face in the dark. "Well why did you say that?"

Verna sniffed. "Because you were acting like it is my fault, you were very mean."

I lay back down. "I know" I said "I'm sorry."

I felt the heavy blanket on me again, the guilt pressing down. I was never going to get out from under this, I didn't know how.

And then Verna said something. Something strange that sent a shiver all through my body.

CHAPTER THIRTY-NINE

Dreams in the daytime

My voice was faint "What—what did you say?"

Verna spoke again, louder this time. "Willa said it wasn't your fault."

I opened my mouth and shut it again. Swallowing I tried again, my words floating up like wisps of cotton from my dry mouth. "Willa said—Willa said it wasn't my fault?"

"Yes." Verna's voice was matter of fact.

I said "But when did she tell you that?"

"After she fell." Verna said this like it was no big deal.

I felt dizzy with the thoughts spinning through my head, like I had been twirling around in circles. "But…you never saw her after she fell, and anyways she was dead."

Verna said "I know."

I waited. I dreaded and longed for whatever Verna had to tell me.

Verna finally spoke. "It was in my dream."

I said "You had a dream that night?"

Verna said "No, it was during the daytime. Important dreams happen when you are awake."

"Will you tell me about it?" I could only whisper the words.

Verna said "I stay at home when you take your Dad and the sheriff to the canyon. I still stay there when they take Willa away in the ambulance.

I tried to remember seeing Verna after Willa fell. I couldn't.

She continued. "When you come back to the house and everyone is talking to you, asking all the questions, I just stay in our room and I don't come out. Then just before it is getting dark, I walk down to the canyon and I climb up and sit on the picture rock."

I squeezed my eyes shut. I didn't want to think about picture rock.

She continued. "I sit up there for a while and I am just thinking about my grandmother and I am thinking about Willa, and I am wondering why there are so many people I know that are dying. And then I am wondering if Willa and my grandmother are in the same place." Verna's voice was low and I strained to hear her. "I am thinking that my grandmother will be nice to Willa if she is sad." Verna sat up, hugging her sleeping bag covered knees. In the faint moonlight I watched her motion with her hand, passing it gracefully across her face and up in the air. "Then I have the dream."

Please oh please. My heart was beating so hard. *I don't know if I can take this.*

In the dim light she seemed to be staring off in the distance, through the tent. The Missies slept on. The campfire that had burned down to embers cast a faint glow outside the tent.

Verna said "Willa and my grandmother are standing on the picture rock at the top of the canyon wall. They are looking out and they don't know I am there—they can't see me behind them. " Verna's tone was low and rhythmic, a storytellers voice. "It is the first time I see my grandmother since she died. She looks different, she is young—like my sister Carolyn. Her hair isn't white any more. It is black and hangs down her back. I see her hold out her hand and Willa grabs on to it." Verna raised both arms in the air and said, "They raise their arms high like this and they jump." Closing my eyes the scene sprang to view, clear as crystal.

Verna said "Their jump is far but it looks like it is happening very slow. They hang in the air and Grandmother's hair is straight behind her like a flag. I am shouting at them, but they don't hear me. Then they quit falling because they are changing into hawks. Their arms spread into wings and they flap in a big circle together. I watch them turn, gliding down over the creek. Then they fly back up to me. I am still standing on the picture rock and I reach out my hands. They fly by me on both sides, and their wings touch my fingers."

I realized I had been holding my breath and took a gulp of air. I tried to say Verna's name but no sound came out. I cleared my throat and tried again.

"But Verna—what does it mean? I... I don't get how you know... how Willa told you..."

I quit talking because Verna crawled out of her sleeping bag and kneeled down in front of me. She pressed her fingers on my mouth. "It is my dream. It comes to me because my grandmother knows I will understand it. Part is for me and part is for you. This is your part." Verna put her hand to my ear and whispered. "Willa says it is not your fault."

I pulled my sleeping bag over my face; I pulled up my knees and curled my body toward Verna. I closed my eyes and I was on picture rock again, I saw Willa's excited face, felt her hand in mine.

CHAPTER FORTY

Telling

I started crying again, but not with the desperation of the past months. After a few minutes I got up, made my way out of the tent and cried my way past the glowing coals of the campfire and into my parent's tent. I cried when I heard my Dad ask, "Who is it, is that you Effie?" I cried as I climbed right down into their double sleeping bag between my Dad and Mom. I cried as I remembered everything and told everything that I remembered. I admitted it all. I told them every-single-thing. I cried and they held me and listened, accepting it all, soaking up my grief and guilt. Taking it in. Taking it away.

CHAPTER FORTY-ONE

Summer

I braced myself for summer without a friend. All the adults must have got together to plan how to keep me busy. My Aunt Cleone owned the Juniper Motel and gave me a cleaning job. I worked hard for three hours every morning except Sunday. I got paid $1.60 an hour because there was a brand new minimum wage law. Aunt Holly called me a couple times of week and asked me to "tend" the missies so she could get something done. I would have done it for free, but she said "Believe me, it is worth fifty cents an hour to get them out of my hair for a couple hours." It was nice to be in Willa's home without feeling like I was bugging anybody. It made me feel close to her. Because of these two jobs, I had more money than I had ever had before. Mom made me put half in the bank, but after I did that and paid my tithing, I was still rich. I bought makeup with it, enough to make Verna jealous.

She sent me one letter in July.

Dear Effie. how are you doing? I am fine I have ben mostly helping with the sheeps but on Saturday we went to the rodeo in Window Rock it was the all Indian rodeo so there was no white cowboys. One bullrider got druged around after he got buked off becuz his hand was stuk and he was unconshus. Dont kiss to many boys. From Verna

CHAPTER FORTY-TWO

Another monday

I woke up cold because cover stealing Verna was back. Giving the quilt a yank I curled up on my side. The first day of Junior High and Willa was not going to be coming with me. It was a relief to wake up and remember that she was gone and not be shocked by it. I thought about how I was going to be riding the bus clear across town, miles from the grade school that had been my home since kindergarten. I got up so I could get the bathroom first. After a quick bath I followed the check-list I had prepared the night before: deodorant, lotion, Baby Soft perfume, curling iron. I looked in the mirror. My hair had grown out some over the summer; it was starting to cover my ears a little. A nervous wave flipped in my belly. Junior High, this was big. Lotioned, deodorized and hairsprayed, I came back in the bedroom and start getting dressed.

Verna was awake and asked" What are you gonna wear?"

I showed her my denim skirt, white tee shirt and crocheted vest.

Verna said "That looks pretty good."

I said "What are you going to wear?"

She got out of bed and went to an outfit hanging neatly in the closet, a red and yellow striped shirt and brand new bellbottom jeans.

I said "That will look really cute on you. If you hurry you can get the bathroom before Jimmy Scott does."

When the family gathered for breakfast I was so glad to see Swedish pancakes that I went up and hugged my Mom. She put the syrup on the table. "What's that for?"

I said "For making my favorite breakfast."

Swedish pancakes were thin and sweet, not puffy like regular pancakes, made with lots of eggs. If we were conceited like the Le Large family, we would call them crepes. I held the family record for eating thirteen at one time. Today I felt starved, but started out with five, buttering each one and covering the stack with thin zigzags of syrup. I was so thirsty I drank two tall glasses of milk. Five pancakes was all I could manage and I was finished long before Verna.

After breakfast we rushed around finding our new notebooks and pencils. Mom warmed up the car and gave Jimmy Scott, Verna and me a ride up to Aunt Holly's for pictures. Gussie and Lizzie had insisted that we have a picture taken with all of us together on their first day of "real" school.

Gussie and Lizzie were on the front lawn, jumping up and down with ants in their pants. They were matching, in white blouses with puffy sleeves under purple jumpers with big white buttons on the shoulders. Both sets of faces were scrubbed shiny and two curly ponytails were tied with purple ribbons. By the end of first recess all Aunt Holly's hard work would be down the drain.

Gussie and Lizzie ran over to Verna and me. "C'mon, we've got to take the picture fast or we'll miss the bus," Lizzie was as high as a kite with nervous energy. I felt sorry for every first grade teacher with a whole classroom full of Gussies and Lizzies.

"Okay, okay, we're ready."I said, letting Gussie drag me by the hand. We stood at the front door, the usual spot for first day of school pictures in Willa's family. Jimmy Scott was in the middle, with Verna and me on either side. Gussie and Lizzie stood in front of the three of us.

Aunt Holly put her Kodak Instamatic to her eye and backed

up until she had us all in the picture. "Lizzie, you have got to hold still or I'll never get this done. Okay, that's better. Now say cheese."

Later, when Aunt Holly developed her film she gave us a copy of this picture. Jimmy Scott is smiling, looking handsome and tall, so much like Dad. I am smiling slightly, my head high, staring straight at the camera. Verna is on Jimmy Scott's left, her chin down, eyes peeking out under her long black bangs. Her lips are pressed together over her teeth. Gussie and Lizzie aren't looking at the camera, and they aren't saying cheese. Their eyes are wild, their mouths are open and their faces are turned in the direction of their outstretched arms, both pointing toward the bus they have just spotted coming up the road.

"I think I better take another one," Aunt Holly put the camera to her eye again.

"No!" Gussie and Lizzie screamed frantically. "You'll make us miss the bus, we can't miss the bus!"

As they gathered up lunch boxes and supplies, I slipped away inside the house and went through to the back yard. I ducked under the cottonwood tree, and knelt down by the garbage can lid. The mud was smooth and Willa's footprints were gone, in spite of the Missie's efforts. I had been following Willa's footsteps all my life, and I still wasn't used to being without her. I carefully put the lid back down, stood up, took a big breath and went back to the front yard.

The bus was coming around the bend. Jimmy Scott bent down and gave Mom a quick hug. Mom turned to Verna, and hugged her, "I'm so glad you came back this year Verna. We love having you here." Verna nodded, and looked down and said "Thanks, I'm glad too." Mom looked pleased.

Mom gathered me in a tight squeeze and held on for a moment. Her mouth was at my ear. "Now Effie, you watch out for Verna today. She is so shy. She's going to need you." Then she pulled away and put both hands on my face and looked straight in my eyes. "Effie honey, you're going to be alright. I know you will."

The bus pulled up with a whoosh of brakes , the door folding open. Verna and I walked like grownups across the lawn behind Gussie and Lizzie who ran like lunatics, crashing into Jimmy Scott who was about to get on the bus. Jimmy Scott turned around stepped out of the way and said, "Jeez Louise, take it easy." The Missies climbed on and I followed them up the steps with Verna behind me.

Gussie and Lizzie went about halfway back and found a seat. They began bouncing up and down, wildly waving their arms at us. Lizzie reached over and smacked the vinyl seat in front of her. "Over here guys, we saved you a place."

I made my way up the aisle and slid into the seat being guarded by the Missies.

Verna sat down beside me.

THE END

ACKNOWLEDGEMENT

The lyrical cover art was created by my son, Joey Eddington. He knows this story so well, both where it comes from and how much it means to me. He pulled the image of two hawks soaring through a blue Arizona sky straight from the heart of the book. Thank you for giving Willa her wings.

ABOUT THE AUTHOR

Laraine F. Eddington

Born on a ranch in Arizona, Laraine has been consuming books since she first opened her eyes to the world. Like every writer, she is passionate about reading.

When Willa Fell is set in the world she knew well growing up, northern Arizona's high desert plateau. It is home to fierce wind, vast cattle ranches and hard working people. Her hometown was surrounded by the rich culture of the Navajo, Hopi and Apache tribes. Laraine has great respect for their traditions, as well as a love for the stark beauty of reservation lands.

Without humor, life isn't worth living and writing isn't worth reading. Laraine is fond of the ridiculous and requires a healthy dose of daily laughter. You will find a ripple of wit through all her work.

Laraine loves to hike and hand-quilt while listening to audio books She lives with her husband in Mesa, Arizona, sharing their property with occasional roadrunners and coyotes, but not the cartoon kind.

BOOKS BY THIS AUTHOR

The Rifle

No one dreams more fiercely of owning a rifle than a farm boy in the 1940's. But striving is sometimes sweeter than obtaining. And nothing is more final than a well aimed bullet.
A short story.

Flora, An Environmental Romance Novella

Whether you enjoy romance novels for their own sake, or for the blush producing giggle factor, this romantic parody is for you. Young forest ranger Flora is both alluring and innocent. When danger and love invade her woodland sanctuary, she tries to protect both her heart and her furry forest friends.

Meant to be read aloud, by candlelight, in a silken robe, bubbly beverage in hand.

THANK YOU

It has been my dream to get this story
out of my head and into the world.

Thank you for reading.
I would love to hear from you.

https://laraineeddington.com

Made in the USA
Las Vegas, NV
04 January 2022

40237694R00105